Also by Laura J. Kendall

Hurricane Deadly - Novella

Dedicated to all the first responders, who risk their lives every day, in the quest to save others.

## Acknowledgements

A big thank you to Elizabeth Botel for proof reading and spotting errors I couldn't see! You rock!

I'd like to give a big shout out to all my readers. I appreciate each and every one of you. Your support means the world to me! I'd love to hear from you!

The state of Florida for hosting a big part of this novella. I did my best to make it as genuine as possible, but I must confess, I've never visited the area in person, only on google :)

# A Simple Case of Betrayal

# CHAPTER ONE

The body washed ashore at high tide onto one of Delray's most beautiful beaches. This beach was the back door of a very exclusive community on Florida's south shore. The corpse lay stretched out grotesquely on the fine white sand, bloated and blue with bits and pieces of flesh gorged out by fish, enjoying a late night snack.

She shook her full head of red hair, pulled back neatly in a long pony tail and gazed out the window at the large crowd of wealthy residents, pointing at the body. They all turned in unison to look at her, as she slammed the door shut to her department issued Ford Bronco and all six feet of her started walking down towards the scene.

Deputy Lana Turner hadn't been on the force but two years and the last five months had been hell between bodies of young girls washing up all over the beaches and the pissed off, rich as hell, residents who lived in the exclusive estates. To say they were pissed was an understatement.

A buff man, who looked like he'd stepped off a military special ops mission, charged up the beach right at her and stopped halfway, waiting for her to reach him. Yeah, God forbid the wealthy twit strain his gluteus maxims walking so far. She spit on the ground and arranged her face in a most pleasant manor, getting ready for the onslaught of criticism and anger coming her way.

She walked gingerly as sand practically leaped into her black shoes. Damn it, she knew she should have worn her boots today. She smiled pleasantly as she stopped before the bald man, who height wise, came up to her chest. She held a snarl back as he smiled looking her right in the large breasts.

"Deputy Lana Turner," she held out her hand which he didn't bother to take. Finally he looked up from her chest with a wild gleam in his eyes.

She frowned and the gleam disappeared.

"My name is Mike Kendall. I'm ex navy seal and current special agent with NCIS. Looks like the fish really had a feast on this one."

He turned quickly, looking back at the rotting corpse, but not before she saw a ghoulish grin fill his mouth. Great, just what she needed another wealthy nut job who thinks he's a special agent. Geez!

"Thank you for your observations Mr. Kendall." Walking past him, she felt his hand wrap around her bicep. Instinct kicked in and she grabbed his arm twisting it as she hurled him down hard onto the sand. She pointed at him. "Touch me again and I'll lock your sorry ass up."

Mike Kendall smiled as he looked up at her statuesque frame. He nodded and slowly got to his feet, brushing sand off his crisp blue jeans. "You are one tough chick. I'm sorry about that, I didn't mean to scare you. I was only trying to tell you that I'd like to be addressed as Special Agent Mike Kendall."

She brushed by him not addressing him as anything and made her way through the crowd. "Please step back folks. This is a crime scene."

She glanced back at the parking lot as two more Delray cruisers pulled in and parked next to her beat up Bronco.

She scoped out the area around the corpse, looking for any evidence that hadn't been stomped to death by the wealthy irate citizens. When nothing caught her eye, she turned to face the grim reality of the bloated body lying at her feet.

Grimacing, she leaned in closer and really took in the devastation. Clumps of brunette hair stuck out of the cracked skull, which was bashed and crushed in multiple places. Eyeless sockets gazed up at her, set in a face or what was left of a face. Hell, she'd seen three of the other bodies and none were as mangled as this one.

"Shit," she mumbled as she squatted down. The women had obviously been beaten and then munched on by the local residents of the sea, but no way had they chopped off her hands with the precision of a sharp blade.

She stood up just as one of the other deputies pushed his way through the crowd. "Back up folks, this is a crime scene," he said forcefully. The crowd seemed to take more notice of a male telling them to move it and they walked away mumbling about the incompetence of their local sheriff department.

"What do you have movie star?" he said jovially.

"Well Deputy Hung Like a Church Mouse, we have a dead body that's washed up on the beach of some very wealthy and pissed off residents.

"Ouch, now that's not what you said the other night about my manly equipment." He bent down next to the corpse. "Ah, hell this one looks worse than all the others put together."

"That's what I was thinking." She bent down even with him. "And the other night was amazing. I was only kidding."

He winked as another deputy strolled over to them. "Will you two lust birds stop cooing at each other? We look bad enough to the locals as it is."

"Good morning Deputy Torres." Rourke Morgan extended his hand and Torres shook it. "Looks like we have another murder victim here, but something is off. Not the same as the others."

Torres nodded, scanning the body and the area around it. "Much more damage to the face and hell what happened to the hands?" He knelt down. "This isn't from any kind of fish." He looked closer. "Holy hell the hands have been severed cleanly."

Deputy Morgan nodded. "Guess we better notify the feds."

Deputy Turner scanned the crowd. "There was  some muscle bound jerk here, just a minute ago, claiming he was with NCIS. He actually grabbed me and I had to take him down." She squinted her light green eyes. "Now where the hell did the little shit go?"

Morgan glanced up and down the beach. "Yeah I saw you talking to him. I thought he fell down and you were helping him up. Did he give you some trouble?"

"Nothing I couldn't handle." Lana rubbed her forehead with her gloved hand. "Said his name was Kendall or something like that."

Torres walked away, griping his radio mic.

Deputy Morgan sighed loudly. "This case is really starting to get to me. So many women are being killed, and this one tops them all!"

Lana nodded. "Let's go for a beer after work ok?"

Rourke smiled. "As long as you don't mock my manly gifts."

Torres stomped back over to them. "Feds are on the way. Lead agent is flying in this afternoon. Name's Oliver

Collins. Until then this scene stays secured."

Lana and Rourke both groaned in unison.

"The body is going to stink up the entire beach by the time the FBI arrives. Glad it's their case!" Torres pulled out the yellow crime scene tape and the group went to work securing the area.

# CHAPTER TWO

Mike glanced, up a frown covering his worn out face as Agent Collins rushed into his office. "Hey Oliver what's up?"

"Hi Mike," he grimaced. "You look like hell!"

"Thanks for the reminder. What can I do for you?"

"I just got a call to go to Delray, Florida, on a murder case. Five bodies of women, ages 20 to 35 have washed up in the area the last few months. They've been working the serial killer angle, but today a whole different animal washed up on an exclusive beach."

"I don't mean to knock down your excitement, but what does this have to do with me?" Mike leaned back in his chair and propped his feet up on his dark cherry desk.

Oliver held up his finger and quickly dropped his brief case on the desk; narrowly missing Mike's scuffed up black boots. He unlocked it and pulled out a manila envelope. "Take a look for yourself." He tossed the envelope to Mike.

Mike dropped his feet to the floor and scooped up the envelope. He opened it and pulled out a series of pictures which he laid out on his desk.

Olive stood back watching Mike's face, which went from studied confusion, to eye opening holy crap recognition.

Mike tapped the pictures. "That's... that's Kay Hunter. I know her head is bashed in, but it's her. I'm sure of it. You think he killed her?"

Oliver leaned forward and tapped a small area on the picture. "See anything else?"

Mike's eyes narrowed as he looked at the picture. "Looks like a tattoo? Some type of symbol. I don't remember her having a tattoo."

Oliver nodded. "She didn't have one when you saw her, but get this, the last place we've been able to trace her and Gas too, was a little tattoo parlor in Mexico City. My agents down there got a positive ID and a picture of the tattoo she got."

"That son of a bitch! I thought he needed her money to survive?" Mike rolled back his chair and stood up.

"He had plenty of his own money, but yes he did need her millions to disappear and somehow he got them." Oliver shook his head. "We just discovered two accounts we didn't know she had. They both contained five million each and they've been cleaned out, as of this morning."

"And Kendall slept with him. I mean shit, my girlfriend... I mean former, girlfriend fucked a psychopathic murderer ..."

"Mike I know you are hurting, but please stop!" Oliver looked up into Mike's watery eyes. "I need you Mike. I need you to hold it together so we can nail this guy once and for all and stop these murders!"

Mike shrugged his shoulders. "Why do you need me? You are the FBI Oliver."

"Yes I am and the FBI has to follow certain rules and regulations, but you and the Midnight Riders Security Inc don't. Get my drift?"

"Don't tell me you are asking me to go with Kendall down to Florida, to work undercover?" Mike started walking towards the door. "No way man! That's not gonna happen." He stuck his head out the office door. " Kipp can you come into my office?" Mike called out.

Kipp Kulani looked up from his desk and nodded.

"Kipp can go with you Oliver. He's a good man for the job." Mike sat down in his leather chair and folded his hands on top of the desk.

"What's up boss?" Kipp extended his hand to Oliver. "Good to see you again Agent Collins."

Oliver smiled. "Same here Kipp and please call me Oliver."

Mike looked up at the two men and smiled slightly. "Kipp I'd like you to accompany Oliver down to Delray Florida. There is a serial killer running amuck, who we believe is Gail Gas/Chris Hawthorne and Oliver wants our agency to assist."

Kipp frowned. "Assist the FBI? Just how will we be doing that Oliver?"

"Midnight Riders isn't tied to rules like I am in the FBI. I want you to do some reconnaissance and get in good with the local police. I don't have to tell you how much the locals hate it when the FBI marches in to take over their investigation."

Kipp nodded. "True." He looked down at Mike. "I'll go only on one condition."

Mike's eyebrows rose up in surprise. "Oh really and what might that be?"

Kipp looked Mike squarely in the eyes. "You are coming with me. It has been unbearable working here with the tension between you and Kendall. Getting away from this mess will do you good, my friend."

Mike sighed deeply and looked down at his unpolished black combat boots. He sat silently for a few minutes and then looked up. "Deal, but I'm not telling Kendall she's staying home to run the shop."

Oliver waved his hand. "No worries, I will tell her and do so without hurting her feelings and worsening the situation between you two."

"Now that I'd like to see." Mike stood up quickly. "So when do we leave?"

Oliver pointed to the clock on the wall. "When the little hand is on the three and the big hand is on..."

Mike punched his arm. "Funny Collins. I'm going to go home and pack and you should do the same Kipp." Mike pulled his black MRI Jacket off a hook and strolled out the door."

"Be at Teterboro by three sharp. I have a private Jet waiting to take us to Florida, without all the customs bull shit."

"Cool," Kipp said as he followed Mike out the door and down the stairs.

Oliver closed Mike's door and followed.

# CHAPTER THREE

Kendall tossed and turned with the usual nightmare, since Chris Hawthorne had disappeared. She rolled right off the bed, falling with a thud, onto the carpeted floor. She grabbed her head as she sat up slowly. "Oh hell."

Bela jumped off the bed and nudged Kendall with her wet nose.

"Ewww! Get off me dog! I don't need your help thanks!" She pushed Bela away with her hand and stood up. Fear and regret permeated her very soul and she didn't know how to escape. "Sorry Bela girl I don't mean to take it out on you."

Kendall walked out to the kitchen, wearing only a ripped tee shirt and panties. "Let's get you some breakfast, girl." Kendall knelt down by Bela's cabinet and opened the doors. She ripped opened a bag of biscuits and pulled three out. "Here you go sweetie."

Bela took them from her and sadly wandered off into the living room. Being a dog she was much more in tune with feelings than humans ever would be. She knew her person was hurting very deeply and there was nothing she could do about it. Plopping down on the carpet, she dropped the biscuits from her mouth and lay her head down, not bothering to eat.

Kendall made herself a cup of tea and rye toast. She sat down at the kitchen table, nibbling at the toast, without really tasting it. When she wasn't scared out of her mind that a psychopath was coming to get her, she was racked with grief over the damage she'd done to her relationship with Mike. If only she could go back and do things differently.

Her cell phone rang from her purse, which was sitting on the floor, by the couch. She didn't bother to get up and answer it. The last thing she wanted to do was talk about this crap called her life, again.

She heard a car pull into the driveway of her new rental home, in Sparta, NJ. Bela jumped up and ran to the door wagging her tail in anticipation.

Kendall shook her head. "Must be one of my do gooder friends again." She stood up and walked into the living room, peeking out the window. Bobbie's Candy Apple Red, Trans Am sat idling in the driveway. She watched the beautiful blonde hang up her cell phone and slide out of the aging muscle car.

Kendall opened the door and stood waiting for her best friend.

Bobbie strolled up the sidewalk and half smiled at her friend. "Why didn't you answer your phone Kendall? I've been calling you since yesterday."

Kendall frowned and shrugged. "Probably because I don't feel like talking, since my life has gone into the shitter and there's nothing I can do about it." She closed the door behind Bobbie, who stomped into the house like she owned it.

Bobbie turned and looked Kendall directly in the eyes. "I've tried to be a good friend and be there for you, but this has gone on for long enough." She pointed at the sofa. "Sit down and let's figure this out. You need some professional help."

Kendall plopped down on the couch and shook her head. "No way! I'm not going to a shrink. All they want to do is put people on medication and numb their brains so they can't think anymore. No thanks!"

Bobbie sat down next to her and reached out for her hand. "Honey I'm not talking about a shrink."

Kendall looked up. "No? Than what are you talking about?"

Bobbie slipped a business card from the back pocket of her denim jeans and handed it to Kendall. "I've scheduled you an appointment for today at 3:00 pm."

Kendall read the card with her eyebrows raised as she tapped her right foot on the carpeted floor. "A life coach? What the heck is a life coach?"

Bobbie got up and walked into the kitchen. "A life coach is someone who helps you see just how powerful you really are. They don't give advice and they don't snow you on medication. They partner with you and empower you to take control of your life and take action." Bobbie yanked open the fridge door and pulled out a can of sweet tea. "I've gone to her for the past six months and she's made an amazing difference in my life."

Kendall cocked her head to one side as she watched Bobbie walk back into the room and set down a can of sweet tea in front of her. Bobbie then sat down on a plush chair opposite of hers. "You've had a life coach?"

Bobbie nodded. "You know how miserable I was after Chris cheated on me and I divorced his sorry ass. I realized I just couldn't stand one more minute, of one more second, living with the thoughts rolling around in my head, from morning to night. I didn't want a shrink either, but I wanted a change. That's when I found an ad for my life coach. It's been amazing and I have come out on the other side of doom and gloom and grief, into a life I am genuinely starting to enjoy again."

Kendall leaned forward and squeezed her friends shoulder. "I have noticed a change in you and I've actually been wondering how you worked through everything that happened." Kendall stared down at the card as her eyes teared up. "I don't think I can stand one more minute, of one more second, of this hell that has become my life. I'll go. Thank you Bobbie."

Bobbie got up and sat down next to Kendall on the couch. "Girlfriend I'm here for you. Take this step and it will make an amazing difference."

## CHAPTER FOUR

He smiled as he watched the stupid cops standing around what was left of Kay's body. Bunch of friggen idiots. He was way too smart to ever be caught by the likes of them. He licked his lips as the tall red head with giant tits bent down to pick something up from the sand. It glittered in the sun as she handed it to the darker skinned deputy. Worry shot through him momentarily as they turned as a unit and looked directly at him.

Tits and ass nodded his way as she said something to the other cops. He backed away into the palm trees surrounding the private beach. Time to beat feet and boogey. Behind him he heard shouts and someone running his way slowly through the heavy sand.

He scooted out from behind a palm tree and dove into the ocean. The boat was moored only a half a mile away, which was an easy swim for him. He dove under the waves so the cops couldn't see him.

Not like they were going to dive in with their spiffy uniforms and shinny boots. His mind twisted onto the red head as he held his breath, swimming under the water. Now that bitch he'd like to have tied up and wet and ready for him. He shot to the surface and took a quick breath before diving down again. She'd probably put up a good struggle, all the more to turn him on. He shook his head and just for a moment a measure of his weakness came to him. He remembered the only time he'd ever really cared about a woman and she'd mocked and snubbed him. Of course that had been during his Gail Gas days. Now the whore would probably be all over his muscle bound ass.

His lungs were screaming as he rose slowly to the surface and paused long enough to look back at the shore. Hell, had he been imagining the whole thing? The cops were all standing around Kay's carcass and didn't appear to be looking for him at all.

The boat was moored a short distance away from where he surfaced, so he swam over to the ladder and climbed on board. Now his boat, thanks to Kay and the money he'd gotten her to sign over to him, before he'd gotten rid of her.

His cock grew hard, filling up his dark blue Speedo as he pictured Kay down on her knees, begging for her life. He slipped his hand down and around his throbbing cock and slowly moved it up and down the thick shaft.

He lay down in the front of the boat on the dark red cushions and pulled the Speedo off. Working his cock, he remembered how Kay had gagged on his long dick, when he'd rammed it in and out of her mouth. He'd pulled her hair so hard a patch of it had come out in his hand. His milky white cum had flooded her mouth just that moment. He'd pulled his cock out and snapped her neck like a tooth pick, with his bare hands. She'd fallen face first, dead on the wooden floor, with his cum drooling out of her useless orifice.

His load shot all over his hands and stomach. Standing up he dove off the bow into the warm water and washed off. Climbing back onto the boat he strutted around naked and glistening in the warm sun. He felt like God in the flesh.

Pulling out a pair of binoculars he sat down in the driver's seat and panned the shore line. More cops had shown up, including the forensic division. Not like they'd find anything with the precautions he'd taken. He'd set the scene just right so the FBI would get involved. If the FBI was involved than Kendall would be too. He couldn't wait to see her in person again. Smiling, he imagined the horror on her face when he would put his plan into effect and take her all for himself.  Starting up the engine he drove off, delighting in the warmth of the sun playing on his nude body

## CHAPTER FIVE

Mike and Kipp met Oliver at Teterboro Airport and they walked out to a waiting plane, together. Oliver climbed the steps first, with Mike following.

"Wow, the FBI sure doesn't skimp on the jets they fly you hotshots around in!" Kipp took in the elegant décor- set in tan, rich brown, white, and black shades of color.

Oliver smiled. "Just one of the perks my friend." He waved his hand around the plane. "Feel free to sit anywhere you want, we are the only ones on this leg. We may have some company on the way back, but we'll see how that plays out.

Mike sat down in a plush, tan leather seat and placed his brief case underneath the it. "Flight should be about two hours, right?"

"Yes sir," Oliver said. He walked over to the mini bar and opened the fridge. Pulling out a can of coke, he held it up in the air. "Either of you care for a beverage?"

Mike shook his head. "What no hot flight attendants?" He looked Oliver up and down. "The least you could do is wear something a little sexier, this is your job we're talking about here."

Oliver grimaced as Mike laughed and Kipp rolled his eyes. His insecurities cropped up for just a minute, but he pushed them down and fell into the spirit of the game.

Oliver curtsied as he handed each of the men a glass, filled with ice and a can of coke. "Here you go, handsome."

Mike raised his eyebrows. "U'm."

Oliver turned beet red. "Oh no ... not like that.."

Mike smiled. "Man, you are so easy. Gotcha."

Oliver exhaled loudly. "No fair, don't do that to me. I thought you were serious."

"Well I am pretty cute." Mike sipped his coke and leaned back in the seat. "So seriously, what is our game plan, once we land?"

Oliver sat down across from Kipp and Mike. "First we go by the crime scene and check out what's left of it and then we have a pow wow with the local deputies, to find out what's been going on."

"What do you think is going on? I'm sensing there is something you aren't telling me." Mike wagged his finger at Oliver.

Oliver grimaced. "The locals aren't exactly doing a great job at figuring this one out."

Mike leaned forward, anxious for the truth. "And…"

Oliver looked him directly in the eyes. "And I believe it is our little friend out there, wreaking havoc on the shores of the elite and famous. So I need you both to get in real good with the local deputies."

Kipp nodded and set his drink down in the seat holder. "I was afraid you were going to say that. Just how good is real good, Oliver?" He clicked on his seatbelt as the plane started to taxi down the runway. "Cause I only go one way, if you know what I mean."

Oliver laughed. "What, you won't take one for the team Kipp? How about you Mike?"

Mike turned beat red and Kipp spit coke out, all over the plush carpet.

Oliver leaned back in his seat smiling. "You guys are so easy. Gotcha!"

Mike smiled until he realized the jet was gaining speed as it shot down the runway. He had a death grip on the seat handles as the plane lifted off the ground and took off.

Oliver watched him from across the way and smiled. "Do you think maybe you could have told me you aren't a good flyer?" Oliver leaned forward and pulled out his brief case from under the seat. He popped open the top and reached in, pulling out a prescription bottle. Popping off the top, he jiggled the bottle and a little pill fell out.

Mike closed his eyes, holding onto the arm rests for dear life. He felt a tap on his knee and opened his eyes widely.

Oliver leaned forward. "Hold out your hand." He dropped the little pill into Mike's large hand. "Take this now and it will ease the tension you are feeling. I take one before each flight and see I'm hardly stressed at all."

Mike nodded and popped the pill into his mouth, swallowing it quickly, without anything to even wash it down. He rested his head back on the chair and closed his eyes. A few minutes later the tension that gripped him started to leave. He opened his eyes and exhaled loudly.

Oliver smiled. "See, works like a charm."

Mike smiled. "I don't even care what it was, but can you get me some for the trip back too."

The plane leveled off as it reached its altitude and the three men released their seat belts. Oliver swung a table out from the wall and moved it between them. He pulled up his brief case and set it down on the table, popping open the lid. He pulled out a map and laid it down, spreading it out on the surface.

Mike leaned forward and looked at the map. It had several x marks in bright green color. "What do these stand for?" He pointed to the x's.

"Those are where the bodies have washed up. You can see they have all been within a 20 mile radius. We know that Gas and Kay Hunter took off in a boat and we thought they'd dumped it and flown off to Mexico. Now we aren't so sure."

Mike shook his head. "I swear if I ever get my hands around that piece of shit's neck, I won't stop squeezing until the bastard is dead."

Kipp squeezed Mike's arm. "I can't begin to imagine how you feel Mike. I am so sorry about Dave and Kendall. We are gonna catch this guy and when we do he's all yours."

Oliver sighed. "I can't say I'd stop you."

## CHAPTER SIX

Kendall stepped out of the first hot shower she'd had in three days and pulled a towel off the rack. She bent down and wrapped the towel around her long, feathered blonde hair. It was nearly one o'clock and she had to get a move on it for the three o'clock appointment. Was she really going to do this? She wasn't sure she needed to. After all she'd made it through so much on her own.

She slipped on a pair of blue jeans, brown cowgirl boots and a black pull over long sleeve tee shirt. Letting her hair fall free of the towel she combed it out and applied leave in conditioner. Her phone rang just as she picked up the blow dryer.

Sighing, she looked down and saw Bobbie's number. "Yes, I'm going," she said as she flipped open the phone.

Bobbie laughed. "Ok, just wanted to make sure. You are my best friend and I want you to get your mojo back."

Kendall smiled. "My mojo, huh?" She set down the phone and ran her fingers through her wet hair. "I love you girl and I really appreciate all you are doing for me. Let me dry my hair and I'll be out the door."

"Call me when you get done."

"Will do sista," Kendall said brightly. She hung up the phone and feeling better than she had in a long time, she picked up the hair dryer and began to dry her feathered hair.

Fifteen minutes later she was ready. Bela raced to the door with her and she bent down and kissed her soft yellow face. "Sorry girl, I have to go out, but I promise I'll take you for a walk when I get home."

She walked over to Bela's cabinet and pulled out a few biscuits. "Here you go Bela girl," she said as she set the biscuits down on the floor. Bela raced over and happily scooped up one of the biscuits. She held it in her mouth as she escorted Kendall to the front door. "See you later girl."

It took her forty five minutes to get from Sparta, to the life coaches office, in Wayne. She parked the Firebird in the lot and sat there for a few minutes gathering her thoughts. Taking a deep breath she opened the door and got out.

She glanced up into a blue sky, with a bright yellow sun shining and shivered as a cool breeze hit her. Quickly she entered the building and found the office right away. Before she could change her mind, she opened the door and walked into the waiting area. It was a decision that would finally get her headed back in the right direction. Smiling, the receptionist held the door open and escorted her down a hall and into a well furnished office. Behind the desk a pretty woman with short, spiked gray hair, stood up, extending her hand. "Hello Kendall. My name is Mary Robin and it is so nice to meet you."

Kendall shook her hand and sat down in a chair opposite the desk. Peace settled over her as Mary Robin focused in on her and smiled.

# CHAPTER SEVEN

From the corner of the debarking area, he watched Mike, Oliver and Kipp walk off the plane and into the airport. He craned his neck, looking for her. Rage filled him up inside as it became clear Kendall was not with them.

His eyes narrowed as he slipped on his sunglasses and pulled down his Yankee ball cap. Anger guided his steps as he walked quickly out of the airport and to the ground level parking area.

His brain worked overtime to figure a way to draw her down to Florida. Then he saw his answer, strutting her made up blonde bimbo self to a waiting limo. With just a little bit of help she'd be a dead, literally, ringer of Kendall.

He ran to his rented Bentley and slipped behind the wheel. Backing out, he drove quickly through the parking lot and managed to get directly behind the limo, now pulling away from the curb.

From the glove box he pulled out his gun and placed it between his legs on the seat. Next he reached in and got the silencer, he carried for special cases and this was definitely a special case.

Using his free hand he attached the silencer to the gun and lowered his driver's side window. As the two vehicles approached the exit, he slowly maneuvered alongside and fired a bullet, soundlessly into the rear tire.

Beside him the limo wiggled in the lane then signaled to pull over. Like a good citizen, he allowed the car to move in front of him and then pulled in behind them to offer help.

He could hear the blonde screeching at the driver from the backseat. This one was going to be fun. He smiled as he got out and walked over to the limo driver, who was kneeling next to the flat tire.

"Looks like you have a flat," Gail said.

"Sure does and my client isn't letting me forget it, not for one minute. She's in a real hurry." The driver stood up as the back door opened and the bottled blonde's legs eased out, long and lean and tan.

Up she popped, anger written all over her flawless face. The frown slowly changed to a smile as she glanced at Gail and then at the Bentley, idling behind him.

"Hello, my name is Lorel." She held out her hand which he quickly pulled to his lips and kissed sweetly.

"Lorel, such a pretty name." For a dead girl, he thought. "I am so sorry your car got a flat, but luckily I saw it and stopped to be your knight in shining armor."

Her giggle ran right through him as she flipped her long hair. "I'm not sorry at all," she said looking his buff frame up and down. "Care to give a lady a lift?"

He winked then motioned for the limo driver to get the ladies bags out and place them in the Bentley. He hit the lock button on his key and the trunk flipped open.

Guiding her over to the passenger door, he opened it and gently helped her inside, the luxury car. "I'll be right back after I tip the driver." He shut the door, rolling his eyes as he walked back to the trunk. He handed the driver a fifty dollar bill. "I hate to see anyone lose a fare like this. You have a good day."

The driver smiled and waved a thank you as he walked back to the car and opened the driver's door, getting in behind the wheel.

The blonde leaned over the center console, her huge breast nearly spilling out of her low cut top. "So where to now?"

"I  thought you were in a big hurry to get somewhere? Just tell me where and I'll have you there in two wags of a dog's tail." Queen bitches, like this one, always ate up his southern boy routine and he laid it on thick.

"Suddenly I'm not in such a hurry. Not with handsome company, such as yourself. I don't know your name yet, silly me." She giggled loudly and snorted.

"My name's Mike Kendall. Pleased to make your acquaintance." He leaned over the console and kissed her as he pushed his hand down her blouse and caressed her breast. She kissed him back, hard and deep, just like he was going to be doing, right before he slit her aging throat.

"I think we need to go some place secluded so I can fuck your brains out." She ran her pink tongue over her teeth, then slid her hand down onto his groin, feeling for his package.

He brushed her hand away and smiled. "Well my little sex - vixen I have the perfect place in mind. No touching the goods, until I have you right where I want you - naked and tied up for my pleasure."

"Kinky. I like it." She leaned back in the luxurious seat and closed her eyes. "Mind if I take a little nap to rest up for the fun?"

"Not at all. You just relax and let me take care of everything." Gas put the car in drive and slowly eased the Bentley out into traffic. He waved at the limo driver as he passed.

It took him just under an hour, to get to the abandoned camp ground. He pulled the car behind one of the run down, paint- peeling cabins and shut off the engine. He looked over at the sleeping blonde and smiled. So peaceful were her last minutes of life.

He shook her shoulder. "Wake up, sleepy head, we're here. I think you'll find this place nice and secluded. Especially if you're a moaner." He winked as she smiled then lifted her arms in a stretch.

She looked around the deserted camp ground which clearly had seen better days. "U'm I thought we'd be going to a posh hotel, not some scummy cabin. What kind of girl do you think I ..."

His hand shot forward, grabbing her around her neck and nearly squeezing the life out of her. Nearly, but not quite, yet." He leaned over and opened the passenger door, then using his legs he pushed the semi-conscious woman out. She fell with a thud onto the hard ground and moaned.

He got out and walked over to the trunk which he opened then yanked out her pink suitcases, filled with things she'd never use again. The blonde lay semi - conscious on the ground as he kicked open the cabin door with his foot and threw her bags into the room.

# CHAPTER EIGHT

She watched them get off the private plane, one at a time. Her piercing blue eyes glinted in the strong sunlight, despite her FBI issued aviators.

The first one off looked to be in his late 40's- early 50's, with striking blue eyes, silver hair, mustache and a big gold wedding ring on his left hand. Damn.

The next one off stood about 5'10 with brown hair and was a sharp dresser. Her gaydar was screaming.

The last one off was tall and brooding. He barely spared her a glance as his foot stepped off onto the runway. He wore aviator glasses that nearly matched the ones on her face. His hair was thick, dark and layered back over his ears. His body was to die for. Yes, this one was a keeper.

She walked confidently towards the men. She'd dressed to impress today in a form fitting short white skirt and flowered pink top. The pumps on her feet really showed off  her well toned legs and she never missed an opportunity to do so.

Silver hair extended his hand and she grasped it firmly, to show she wasn't to be toyed with.

"You must be Agent Debbie Crane," he said smoothly. "My name is Kipp Kulani with the Midnight Riders Inc and this is my partner Mike Garcia." He pointed to the stud standing behind him who had a frown plastered on his handsome face.

She watched as he acknowledged her with a nod of his head. "Good to meet you Kipp and Mike." She turned to face the last man. "You must be my counterpart, Agent Oliver Collins."

"Yes maam, at your service." He matched her grip strength with his. "We'd like to go to our hotel first, check in and get refreshed before a briefing."

She nodded. "Absolutely, my car awaits." She pointed to a midnight black Tahoe and walked over to the driver's door. "Hotel is practically across the street. I'll let you get settled and be back there in an hour give or take two or three."

Kipp hopped into the front passenger seat while Mike and Oliver climbed into the back.

She was glad no women were in the group. They always got in the way of the job with their emotional mood swings and prissy ways. No she much preferred the company of men.

"So we do things differently down here, in Florida. You'll be reporting directly to me as the field agent in charge. I'll expect frequent updates on your progress." She tapped her long blood red nails on the wheel. "I'm not a fan of special civilian groups edging in on my cases."

She turned on the signal and shot across two lanes of traffic and into the Hyatt's parking lot. Horns blared as drivers slammed on their brakes to avoid the blacked out SUV. With a lurch and loud screech the Tahoe came to a stop, in front of the lobby doors.

Kipp looked over at the woman behind the wheel. "What the hell was that?" He shook his head and got out without waiting for an answer.

"Agent Crane that wasn't necessary. You don't have to prove your driving skills to us. Geez." Oliver opened his door, got out and walked to the back of the Tahoe. Yanking opening the hatch, he started pulling out their suitcases. "By the way we won't be reporting to you. I've already set that part of the operation up and you aren't the lead in this, I am. This case carries over from a

NJ case we've, he emphasized we've, been working on. There is a serial killer running lose and we believe he just turned up on the sunny shores of Florida.

She snapped her gum. "Oh really? I'll confirm that with my superiors and let you know."

Mike lowered his aviators and sneered at the woman, now turned facing him. "So you're one of those women who think they have to prove they are as good as a man in everything they do, right?"

Her face turned a bright shade of red as she inhaled sharply. "Sorry it's the way I roll. I'll be more careful of you and your friends insecurities next time." She exhaled. "Bunch of pansies from Jersey."

Mike reached forward and went face to face with the blonde. "Lady you have a chip on your shoulder a mile wide. How about you drop it off before you come back here to get us. Oh and by the way, I'm a New Jersey State Trooper honey, so back off with the attitude of us against them."

"Fuck you," she mumbled under her breath.

Mike sat back, then opened the door and got out.  With a kick to the door he slammed it shut. "That one is a real piece of work," he said angling his head at the driver.

"I'll be getting us our own SUV. Don't worry about having to drive with her again." Oliver leaned into the back of the Tahoe. "Be back here in an hour Agent Crane or we'll find someone else to brief us." With that he slammed the hatch door shut.

They each picked up their respective suitcases and walked in through the automatic doors and into the lobby.

Agent Crane smacked the dash with her hand. "Bastards," she mumbled. Yanking  the truck into drive, she hit the gas and shot out of the parking lot.

# CHAPTER NINE

She awoke, tied naked to the bed, spread eagle. Fear coursed through her as she looked up in to the ice cold eyes of the man she now knew was going to kill her.

"Hello pretty Lorel," he said huskily.

She pulled against the chains, wrapped multiple times around her wrists and feet and secured to the wall and bed with thick screws. A tear dropped from her eye, drifting silently down onto the dirty mattress.

"Didn't your mother teach you not to get into the car with strangers?" He picked up a knife and flashed it back and forth in front of her eyes.

"Why are you doing this to me? I don't even know you?" Lorel stopped struggling and locked eyes with the mad man, praying she could get him to see her humanity.

"Nothing personal honey. You are just a means to an end. You're a slut, obviously, but not even sluts deserve to die the way you are about to." A sharp giggle escaped his lips as he dipped the knife lower and slowly started cutting into her skin.

Screams of anguish filled the cabin as he cut his message into her soft feminine skin.

Pain seared into her chest and abdomen, a raw burning like she'd never felt before in her life. "Stop, please stop! Oh my God the pain! Please I'll do anything you want. Please..."

He bent down and looked directly into her water filled eyes. Through her tears she saw him smile as he hefted a huge knife over her chest and then plunged it into her heart. It was the last thing she saw on the earthly plain.

He sat down on the bed and gently caressed the still warm dead woman.

His message was clearly written, no make that carved into the dead blonde, who bore a striking resemblance to Kendall. It was guaranteed to get her to Florida and if she didn't show then many more would go, just like this bitch.

His thirst for killing was rapidly wearing thin. Face it, he was bored as hell and ready to disappear to an island somewhere. Just a few more details to take care of and he'd be free to live the life he wanted.

Standing up he looked down at his latest master piece, then went about making sure the room was set just perfectly for his plan.

Without a look back or one swipe of a cloth to erase his prints he walked out of the cabin and got into the Bentley.

He felt the powerful engine come to life beneath his hands as he put the car in reverse and drove away. It was only a mile or two to a pay phone. Yes, miraculously up in the sticks there still was a pay phone.

He turned up the local hick station and hummed along to the song. Life was good and it was about to get even better.

## **CHAPTER TEN**

Mike looked at his watch for the hundredth time as Oliver hung up the phone.

"Car is on the way. We aren't waiting for Agent piss ass Crane another minute. I've never seen such unprofessionalism in my life!"

Kipp nodded. "She's a winner all right. Let's put this behind us and get to the scene, to figure out what the hell our friend the serial killer is up to."

Mike snorted. "What he's up to? Really, Kipp? Gosh what could it be?"

Kipp and Oliver looked at him with confusion and anger.

"What is your problem Mike? If you didn't want to come to work this case than why didn't you say so." Kipp slipped on his sun glasses and walked out the hotel room door.

Oliver shook his head. "Look I know you've been through a hell of a lot, but taking it out on those who actually care about, you isn't called for." He followed quickly behind Kipp without a look back at the brooding state trooper.

Mike sighed, mentally kicking himself for being such an ass. "Hey guys wait up," he called.

Kipp and Oliver kept walking and stopped at the elevators. Both turned to face the large man, practically running down the hall.

He reached them, just a bit out of breath, which considering his recent injuries wasn't too bad. "I'm sorry. I know I'm wound tight and I'm sorry I snapped at you. I do want to be here and I want to put an end to the sicko as much as you do."

Kipp didn't take off his shades, but nodded.

Oliver smiled weakly. "No harm, no foul. Let's all pull it together and get Gas!"

The elevator door swung open and the men stepped inside. The ride down was silent except for the upbeat elevator music playing overhead.

They exited the elevator and walked outside, just as an unmarked, blacked out FBI cruiser arrived. The agent handed the keys to Oliver and nodded. He got in another waiting car and drove away.

Kipp got into the passenger front, Mike in the rear and Oliver slipped behind the wheel. Creatures of habit.

"The scene is only about 10 minutes from here. My guess is, that is where we are going to find the lovely Debbie Crane," Kipp said. He leaned over and turned up the local rock station.

"I'm sure you're right. I did a little research on her with some of my contacts and she's well known for being a respected and efficient agent, with a huge chip on her shoulder." Oliver put on his blinker as he turned the car right, leaving the parking lot.

"What's got her panties in a bunch?" Mike glared out the smoked window.

"From what I can gather, she's well qualified, but has been passed over for several promotions. She's claiming gender discrimination."Oliver drove the cruiser at the posted speed limit.

"Hell, with how I've seen them treat you Oliver, she's probably right. Gotta be frustrating and now here come the out of town cowboys to take over her big case," said Kipp.

"Makes sense. How about we agree here and now that no matter how much of a bitch she is to us, we cut her some slack?" Mike ran his fingers through his layered hair. "God knows I can sympathize with her."

Oliver and Kipp both said "Deal" at the same time.

"You owe me a beer," said Oliver.

"No way, I said it first," Kipp said.

Mike leaned back in the seat and closed his eyes, smiling. A few minutes later he opened them as the road changed from pavement to sand. He scanned the areas and his eyes immediately found a most unexpected surprise.

He opened his door and stepped out, just as the surprise reached their car. She stood six feet tall and well built, even in a drab deputy uniform. She smiled, flipping back the most amazing, sexy red hair, he'd ever seen. She looked about thirty five, probably a good five or six years younger than Kendall.

She stopped dead in her tracks as he lowered his sunglasses, revealing his azure eyes. He extended his hand. "Hello, I'm Mike Garcia, with the Midnight Rider's Security Team."

She exhaled sharply, clearly as caught up in the new found sexual tension as he was. "I'm Deputy Lana

Turner." She lowered her glasses, revealing light as glass green eyes.

Her grip was strong and firm, just like she was. Mike smiled as he released his hand then pushed his sun glasses back up onto the bridge of his nose. Lana did the same.

Kipp coughed loudly, behind the sex struck couple. "I'm Kipp Kulani, lead investigator for Midnight Riders and this is FBI agent Oliver Collins. You are?"

Lana nodded. "Welcome to our little beach of hell. I'm Deputy Lana Turner. The man in charge from our department is right over there." She pointed to Deputy Torres, who was standing guard over the corpse, now grotesquely melting in the unbearable heat and sun. Beside Torres stood a beautiful blonde, with a big frown on her face.

"Remember, we're cutting her some slack." Kipp shrugged.

"Right, but by the looks of it, that's not gonna be so easy." Oliver shook his head as he stared at the bristling blonde.

Resigned, Kipp and Oliver moved off towards the scene, while Mike and Lana walked together, lagging behind.

A deputy, with just a flash of silver at his temples, stomped up the beach, grimacing. He passed Oliver and Kipp with a quick nod of his head. He didn't bother to introduce himself, clearly intent on going somewhere.

That somewhere was the spot where Lana and Mike stood talking intently. He barged into their private conversation.

"Hey Lana, we could use your help down by the body. Crowds getting a bit out of hand. He held his hand out to Mike. "Hello, I'm Deputy Rourke Morgan."

Mike looked the deputy up and down, aware there was more going on here than met the eye. He looked at Lana, who just barely had a frown on her beautiful lips.

Mike shook the guys hand, eliciting a groan from the deputy. "Nice to meet you. I'm Mike Garcia with Midnight Riders Security Team."

Lana turned to Mike. "Why don't you go and join your team. I have something I need to discuss with Deputy Morgan." She smiled

Mike shrugged and walked away.

Lana turned to the older, but handsome as hell deputy. "Just what was that Rourke?"

He looked away, not meeting her piercing stare. "Not sure what you mean Lana. I'm just trying to get this investigation moving along so we can get the hell off this beach and have that beer you promised me tonight."

Lana shook her head. "You know I hate jealousy and you and I aren't anything more than fuck buddies, right?"

Rourke blushed a deep red. "After last night, you still feel that way?"

Lana nodded as she watched Mike walking away. "I sure do and I'm feeling it more and more each second I stand here, looking at your frown." She turned and followed Mike down the beach.

Rourke stood for a few minutes looking up at the bright blue sky. Lana had the reputation of loving and leaving them, but he'd thought he was different. Now another piece of ass has arrived on the scene and she's off sniffing him. Well, screw her! He turned, his face a mask of calm indifference and walked down to the crime scene.

He joined the group, standing next to a pretty blonde, who filled the air with her take charge voice. Now here was a real woman. Sexy, take charge. He made a mental note to get to know her better.

"Perhaps you can fill everyone in on your case from New Jersey, Agent Collins." She stood ram rod straight. Her eyes locked onto Oliver's.

Oliver nodded. He started from the beginning and didn't spare them any of the gory details. When he finished he looked directly at Agent Crane. Her breathing was rapid and shallow and she looked white as a ghost. "That about covers it, up until Kay Hunter, was discovered by you."

Agent Crane swallowed deeply. "It is very clear that we are dealing with a man who will stop at nothing to destroy you." She waved her finger, pointing at Kipp, Mike and Oliver. "As well as killing innocent people as a means to an end."

Kipp looked down at what remained of Kay Hunter. "It doesn't matter who you are or how you've helped him. If you stand in his way or he is done using you, make no mistake, this is how you will end up."

Agent Crane's phone rang and she stepped away from the group to answer it. She returned two minutes later, shaking her head. "Saddle up boys, our crazy ass killer just left you a message, about an half hour from here."

Mike, Kipp and Oliver looked at her expectantly.

"I don't know anything other than they found a body after an anonymous call was placed to the local sheriff's department. All they will say is it is clearly meant for you."

With that Agent Crane walked up the beach towards her SUV. Kipp and Oliver followed with Mike lagging behind for a moment.

He turned to Lana as she approached his side. "I'd love to see you again, sometime."

Lana winked. "We usually go out after work, around nine o'clock, at the local cop bar - Blue Stingray. I'll hold a seat for you."

Mike smiled. "I'll be there."

As quickly as he could, with his nagging injuries, he raced to catch up to the group, as they climbed into separate SUVs.

Crane, alone in hers, took the lead.

# CHAPTER ELEVEN

Kendall walked out of her new coach's office and straight into Bobbie.

The two women jumped back.

"What are you doing here? Checking up on me?" Kendall smiled at her best friend.

Bobbie didn't smile back. "We have to talk."

Kendall frowned. "What's going on? Is Bela OK?

Bobbie nodded. "Bela's fine, Kendall. Well there isn't any easy way to tell you this, so here goes. " Bobbie motioned for Kendall to sit down in one of the lobby chairs and she sat down next to her.

"Stop with the suspense Bobbie, I don't appreciate it. I'm nervous as it is and this isn't helping."

Bobbie nodded. "I just got a call from Kipp." She exhaled loudly looking down at the floor then back at Kendall. "A woman's body was found in Florida today. She'd been mutilated and stabbed in the chest with a knife."

Kendall held up her hands. "So what does this have to do with me?"

"I'm getting there. It isn't easy. The woman could be your twin and the way she was mutilated was by having words carved into her skin, while she was still alive."

Kendall blanched. "That's horrible. Please don't tell me it's him."

Bobbie leaned forward and took one of Kendall's trembling hands in hers. "It's him honey. The message carved into the woman said; "For each hour Kendall isn't here, another will die."

Kendall sagged in the chair and leaned her head forward, to stop from passing out. "I can't do it. No, please don't make me confront him again. I can't Bobbie."

Bobbie knelt down next to her friend and started to cry. "I'm so sorry, but they have a plane waiting for us as we speak. CJ, Andy, Jerry, Bert and Joe are already at the airport. I've called Bela's pet sitter, so she is taken care of as well. Your bag is packed and in my car."

Kendall looked up into her best friend's tear filled green eyes. "How can you ask me to do this?"

"If I could do it for you I would. It hurts me like hell to see you like this, but if you don't go more will die."

Kendall wiped away tears, now falling like rain. "He's going to win you know. I don't stand a chance against him, not in this state of mind. You are signing my death warrant."

Bobbie's tears ran down her face, makeup smearing beneath her eyes. "You'll die over my dead body and the bodies of everyone on the team. I promise you that." She stood up and held out her hand. "I'll be with you every step of the way."

Kendall took her hand and slowly stood up, her spirit long since sucked from her, by Gail Gas and his abuse. Dejectedly, she followed Bobbie to the waiting Trans Am and got into the passenger side. Bobbie closed the door behind her and walked to the driver's side and got in.

She turned and looked at the shell of her best friend, sitting beside her. "Kendall, sometimes facing our darkest fears are what finally free us. I believe this is your time, to do just that. I'll be with you every single step of the way."

Kendall nodded as tears dripped from her eyes onto her jeans and the aging muscle car drove her away for her safe life and to towards her fate.

# CHAPTER TWELVE

Two hours had passed since they'd been on the scene with the stiff and still no Kendall. "Well you know what that means." He giggled as he picked up the keys to the new Jaguar he'd purchased and headed out the door of his rented hotel room.

He opened the door of the Maroon luxury car and slid onto the plush leather seats. He sat there for a few minutes, taking in the unabashed luxuries this car offered. The finest of everything. The only thing missing was Kendall. He reached over and ran his fingers across the passenger seat where she would soon be sitting.

He inhaled deeply, expanding his well built chest, then popped in the key and started the powerful engine. Life was good.

This next one had to be someone really special. Someone who would cause a real sensation. The radio played in the background, until the local record jockey introduced the latest singing sensation, Dee Dee Reed.

He'd heard her sing live, once. Her hair was blonde and so long it reached past her toned ass. His cock hardened as a plan formed in his mind. This one he was going to enjoy. With his ability to change like a chameleon, she didn't stand a chance.

He turned the car around sharply in the middle of the four lane road, causing cars to screech their brakes and blare their horns. He gave them all the finger by holding his hand up high out his window. If they only knew who they were playing with, they'd happily drive away, with their boring lives still intact.

The radio station was only a few minutes away and he pulled to the curb, just as the announcer said good bye to his prize guest. A black limo idled at the curb, obviously waiting for the star to come down.

He got out of his car and walked over to the limo's driver side window and knocked once.

The tinted window slowly slid down and he shoved his fake cop ID inside. Leaning through the window, he said a few words to the driver, who eagerly opened the door and got out.

Gail held up his finger to his lips and shook his head at the driver who smiled back, nodded and walked away. Quickly he slid behind the wheel and picked up the driver's black cap, sitting on the passenger seat. He slipped it on, adjusting the too big hat on his clean-shaven head.

A commotion sounded as fans shouted and screamed for the beautiful blonde to spare them an autograph or kiss.

He watched through the tinted windows as she rolled her eyes, pushing past her waiting fans. If she only knew they were the last fans she'd ever see, perhaps she might have been a bit nicer.

He tapped the wheel and smiled as a big goon opened the rear door and the blonde slipped inside. Before the goon had a chance to get in on the other side, he gunned the engine and a way they went. The goon ran behind the fleeing limo, screaming for him to wait.

"Hey wait for my body guard, you stupid ass!" The pop singer's furious face filled the rearview mirror. She edged her way up to the front and started to screech at him. He hit the button and the divider slowly went up, separating him from her deafening, high pitched voice.

By the time he was done the country would thank him for ridding it of such a soul sucking diva. He pushed the lock buttons for the back doors and hit the lock down button so she couldn't open them, even if she tried.

Checking and rechecking his side mirrors for the police, who must surely know what had happened by now, he relaxed as it became clear they weren't being followed.

He'd picked out his next place well in advance and had several more just waiting for victims. Turning the limo down a narrow dirt road he drove slowly so as not to kick up a lot of dirt that might alert aerial search units.

A big dilapidated red barn loomed ahead. He stopped in front of it and got out. Opening the big double doors wide, he then got back into the limo and drove it inside. He really relaxed now, knowing that nothing and no one was going to interrupt the fun he had planned.

Shutting off the engine he got out and walked back to close the barn doors. Inside the limo the pop star screamed her indignations. She was gonna be a fireball. He rubbed his hands together in anticipation. Practically skipping backwards, he leaned into the limo and hit the locks off button, essentially freeing the frisky little filly from the back compartment.

She bolted from the passenger side. A very clever move to buy her time to escape, since he was on the other side. He leaped across the roof and dropped efficiently down behind her. She screamed as his arms went around her waist and neck and he brutally threw her to the ground and landed on top of her.

She spit, kicked and tried to claw her way out of his grip, but she was not match for his brute strength and stamina.

He simply sat astride her, holding her arms down with his hands and the rest of her five foot three frame with his torso. After several minutes of flat out screaming and vicious attempts to emasculate him, she stopped fighting. Ah, but this one was far trickier than the others, so he didn't let his grip go as he stood up and yanked her to her feet.

She kicked out with her silver toed boot, connecting with his shin. Enraged anger clouded his thought as all reason left him and he snapped her neck like a twig and she fell limply to the barn floor.

"Fuck!" He kicked the barn wall with his boot. "Damn it! Stupid idiot, you wanted to enjoy this one and what did you do?"

He paced back and forth over top of the body. The blonde's tongue lolled out the side of her mouth and her now sightless eyes looked up at him accusingly.

He bent down and gripped her hair, then dragged her body across the dirt floor over to where a noose swung from a large barn beam. Still same end result, just not as much fun.

He yanked the woman up into his arms and while balancing her he looped the noose over her head and around her neck. Letting go he dropped the body onto the ground and then walked over to the other end of the rope.

With one hard pull the rope squeezed around her neck and yanked her body into a standing position.

"Not a very graceful thing in death are you bitch?" He laughed as her legs half fell out from under her dead weight. He gripped the rope and pulled it hard enough to lift her up and off her feet. She hovered about a foot off the floor as he secured the rope to wooden slat.

From his belt he pulled a knife then walked around in front of the hanging body. With a few strokes, he slashed her clothes which lay cut and crumbled on the ground. Using the sharp point, he carved a big # 2 right above her huge tits. Moving down to her flat belly he carved the one name that meant everything to him.

Standing up his face smacked against her right tit. His cock sprang to life, pounding against his pants. He pulled the tit into his mouth and sucked as he fondled the other hanging globe. He exhaled and walked over to the rope, releasing her body down to a workable level.

Back between her legs, he unzipped his pants and pushed them to the ground. Grabbing the still warm corpse around her waist, he jammed his cock inside her and released his tension and DNA into her hole. Pulling out he hoisted up his pants and fully sated, smiled. Hey, necrophilia wasn't so bad after all. He slapped her bare ass then walked over to the rope, untied it and pulled until the once beautiful blonde swung a full five feet off the ground.

He stayed for just a moment admiring his latest handy work, then exited the barn's rear door and walked across the meadow to where he stashed a dirt bike. With a roar of the engine, he was gone.

# CHAPTER THIRTEEN

Kendall slept the whole way on the plane ride, too exhausted emotionally, mentally and physically to even be her normal, scared- flyer self.

Bobbie sat next to her on one side and CJ on the other, closest to the window.

It was well over three hours later when the plane safely touched down and taxied to the gate.

"Come on honey, it is time to get off," Bobbie said gently.

CJ rubbed Kendall's shoulder. "We're here Kendall. We are all here and we aren't going to leave you."

Slowly Kendall opened her eyes and looked around at her concerned friends. Tears fell again as she nodded and slowly stood up on wobbly legs.

Behind her she heard Joe, Jerry, Bert and Andy talking.

"Look at her. How can we make her do this?" Jerry said.

"We don't leave her side." Bert looked from man to man and each nodded.

Andy stepped up and helped Kendall move out of the narrow seat and into the isle. "I got ya."

Kendall looked up and nodded. "I'm just a hollow shell of who I used to be. Look at me. I'm no good to anyone."

Bobbie moved beside her. "You're good to us. It is time this ended Kendall. He's controlled you long enough. Time to take back your life."

Kendall didn't reply, she simply walked slowly down the aisle and out into the airport. Her friends surrounded her, shielding her from what lay ahead. The truth was nothing and no one was going to be able to shield her from whatever fate had in store. The only one who was going to save her, was indeed herself. Picking up her head she glanced around the airport, watching and waiting for him.

# CHAPTER FOURTEEN

Shock filled his eyes as he watched Kendall or what looked like Kendall exit the plane. This wasn't at all what he expected. She'd lost weight, looked gaunt and her hair and makeup were a mess. No this would not do at all.

He ducked behind a large man as another group walked forward and met Kendall's party. They were all there, with a few new ones added. Interesting, he thought. The game was a foot.

Kipp was the first to wrap his arms around Kendall and hug her. The others followed suit, except for the nasty blonde federal agent and his rival Mike Garcia.

Garcia seemed to shrink in the back of the group, not wanting to meet Kendall's eyes. She merely looked up at him and blinked, then looked away.

What the hell had happened to her in the short time he'd been with Kay Hunter? Was she so distraught he wasn't with her, she'd let herself cave into oblivion?

Behind them he noticed a the big red headed deputy striding towards the group and making a bee line for Mike.

Anger shot through him at the indignity Kendall now faced as the deputy clearly called dibs on Mike.

Mike smiled as the Amazon woman said hello. In fact his face lighted up and he didn't give a shit how it affected Kendall, who stood staring open mouthed at the two soon to be lovers.

Kipp and the others pushed past Mike and his new flame, escorting Kendall away and out of the airport.

"You are truly a piece of shit," said Bobbie as she passed by Mike.

Lana looked at her in surprise. "Honey you talking to me?"

Bobbie stopped short and faced the other woman, nearly four inches and several pounds bigger than her. She stomped back. "Actually I was talking to Mike here, but since you seem to have your ass all up in his, I'm more than happy to include you in that statement too."

Gail nearly clapped out loud as the scrappy blonde took on the Amazon. Kendall had a true friend in that one.

The redhead stepped forward as did Mike who moved between Lana and now Bobbie, CJ and Agent Debbie Crane.

Crane wrapped her arm around Bobbie and whispered in here ear. "Look

I don't know what's going on here, but clearly we are causing a scene and putting Kendall in danger, without a unified front."

Bobbie glared at the agent and then at Mike and Lana. "You're right, whoever you are. Unlike you Mike, the rest of us are putting Kendall and her sanity and safety first. How about you and your big friend here find something else to do, K?"

Lana tried to push past Mike who kept his grip strong and firm on the uniformed deputy. "Lana she's right. Please, let's go somewhere else and you and I work this out."

Agent Crane let Bobbie go and looked up at Mike. "I don't even know what is actually going on here, but even I can tell you are one big loser. Why don't you two go get a room and let the professionals handle the serial killer."

With that Crane, Bobbie and CJ walked away, leaving the stunned couple standing there.

Gas put his hand over his mouth, to stifle the sound of his giggle. Yes, this was going to be fun. Fun indeed and with that his next target was chosen. Kendall would have to wait.

# CHAPTER FIFTEEN

Lana stood there looking first at the women walking away and then at Mike. "Just what the hell was that about?"

Mike grimaced. "I'll be short and sweet. Kendall and I were an item, until Gail Gas fucked her and I mean literally. Of course he was handsome Chris Hawthorne back then, but really how can anyone ever sleep with her, knowing she fucked a serial killer, right?"

Lana started to back away. "I think I best be going."

Mike lowered his head. "I won't blame you if you did. Just know I haven't felt attracted to anyone like I do you." He looked directly into her beautiful green eyes, so different from Kendall's blue ones.

Lana hesitated and with that she leaned forward and kissed him.

Shyly, Mike took her hand and pulled it to his lips. "Thank you."

She winked and squeezed his hand. "My place is about twenty minutes from here. How about you and I go get better acquainted."

"I thought you'd never ask."

They walked out of the airport and to her waiting cruiser. Nineteen minutes to the dot they pulled into her beach front condo's lot and parked. Without a word she got out and he followed her.

Her condo was on the second floor, with wide open ocean views. She pulled him inside, no words needed.

Roughly he removed her duty belt and loaded gun. Then went to work getting her uniform on the floor as quickly as possible.

Lana stood before him naked and built like no other woman he'd ever been with. His cock strained against his jeans, asking for entrance into the fiery love tunnel.

Lana played with her big breasts, pinching the nipples, teasing him until he couldn't take it one more second. He ripped off his jeans. Pulled down his boxer brief, tossing them aside and took her right then and there with his shirt still on.

Like animals in heat, they went at it, exploring every inch of each other's bodies. Tenderly Lana ran her fingers over the scars from his recent and healing injuries.

Each sought relief from the other and both got it. No ties, no love, no commitment, just plain old animalistic sex.

Mike came with a grunt, not having bothered to put on a condom. He pulled out a little too late. His seed spilled into the deputy, who smiled, then leaned forward and kissed him.

"I hope you're on the pill or something!"

"Or something." Lana stood up and let the cum drip down her long tanned legs. She walked outside on her balcony, not caring who saw her naked, amazonic body standing there. Mike followed and bent her over the railing taking her again from behind.

Cheers went up from the beach goers and Mike gave them a thumbs up as he slammed into her raw pussy. He came with another loud grunt then pulled out and walked back inside, flopping down on the couch.

Lana followed him and lay down on top of his half naked body. "Now the neighbors are gonna start talking again, about the sex addict in 3 B." She mused his hair and leaned forward, kissing his lips as her huge breasts slid across his hairless chest. He felt himself grow hard again. Hell, he'd just met her and he couldn't stop screwing her.

What did it matter, his life with Kendall and his career with the Midnight Riders were over. Why not have some fun with a willing sex pot with a real live crotch of fire?

He smiled as he maneuvered his cock and then pushed her down on top of it. She sat up and rocked back and forth, riding him like a stallion.

From the beach below he zeroed in on the law woman's condo and marked its location in his mind, for later on tonight. Oh yes, the fun was about to begin. He laughed as he readjusted his cock in his Speedo and dove into the ocean, swimming for his boat, anchored a short distance away.

# CHAPTER SIXTEEN

The group of friends and inter mixed strangers made their way silently out to the waiting black SUV's, with windows tinted so dark you couldn't see if anyone was inside.

Kipp opened the rear door of one and helped Kendall inside. He eased in beside her and she fell into his arms crying. "How could he do that to me?"

Kipp hugged her back. "I'm so sorry Kendall. I'm at a loss for words.

Bobbie climbed in the other side and took her friend's hand in hers. "He is the ultimate pig!"

CJ turned from the front seat. "I mean really, he's been in Florida for what less than a day and he's already in a trashy red head's pants. Makes me sick!"

"My guess is Mike doesn't care about much other than himself right now," said Oliver.

"What an ass," said Jerry. He shook his head. He rubbed Kendall's shoulder then shut the door and went to the other SUV.

The driver's door opened and much to the men's surprise, Agent Debbie Crane got behind the wheel.

"Oh sorry didn't realize this was your ride." Kipp started to open his door.

Crane leaned back. "It isn't and please don't."

Kipp hesitated as he looked at the blonde behind the wheel.

"Look, I am truly sorry for the way I've behaved. I've wanted a promotion for as long as I can remember and each time a man, not nearly as qualified as me, gets it." When Kipp went to speak she held up her hand. "I'm beginning to realize it changed me into a person I don't like. Can we please call a truce? I really want to help catch this guy, no matter who gets the credit."

Kipp leaned back in his seat as the rest of the group looked at him. "Truce it is Agent Crane."

"Kendall I don't know the depths of what has happened to you, but after witnessing that oaf's behavior back there, I am truly, very sorry."

Kendall nodded with tears rolling down her cheeks. "I used to be so strong and competent. Now look at me I'm a blubbering mess. How am I going to go up against a crazy like Gail Gas?"

"With our help. That's how," said
Bobbie.

Crane put the truck in drive and
headed away from the airport with the
other SUV following.

"I hate to be the bearer of bad news,
but there has been a kidnapping from a
local radio station of a very popular rock
star, named Dee Dee Reed. From the
body guard's description, it sounds like
our man."

Kendall smashed her fists against
the seat on either side of her legs.
"Great, now I've killed another one,
because it took me three hours to get
here!"

"Kendall stop it right now! You
know very well you aren't responsible for
a mad man's actions," Kipp said
authoritatively.

"If you keep thinking that way, you
are never going to rise above the murk
and get your head on straight," said CJ.

"I know you've been through hell
and you are my best friend in the whole
world, but you have to cut this shit out,
now!" Bobbie waited until Kendall looked
her in the eye. "You are still the strong,
competent, kick ass woman you always
were. You've just let Hawthorne, aka

Gail Gas, rent space in it. Time to evict him and take your life back."

Kendall felt the words resonate through her whole body. For the first time in months she felt a spark of her true self. "You are all right in what you say. I appreciate your honesty. I'll do my best."

"That is all we ask." Kipp reached down and squeezed her hand.

Crane's phone rang and everyone went silent. "Oh, okay we are heading there now. Tell them not to touch anything."

She looked at CJ beside her and then glanced in the rearview mirror with a sullen face. "They found Dee Dee Reed hanging naked in a barn, with the number two, carved on her chest and..."

Kendall looked at the rear view mirror grimacing. "Go on, Agent Crane."

"And Kendall, your name carved on her stomach. I'm really sorry." Crane flipped on the lights as did the SUV behind her and together the group raced to the next murder scene.

# CHAPTER SEVENTEEN

Gail Gas waited on the boat, watching the condo. A few minutes before darkness descended, he saw the new couple leave in Lana Turner's patrol car.

"Must be nice to fuck while the tax payers are shelling out money for your salary, Office Fire Crotch." He started the engine and headed for the dock slips, about mile away, where he had another, much larger boat waiting.

Amazing how much Kay Hunter's money was coming in handy. Especially when he paid cash. He still had some last minute alterations to the main cabin to make, before he took her.

He parked the Jag and ambled down the dock and onto a big boat he'd named Swan Dive. It fit, considering what he had in mind for one Deputy Lana Turner. He opened the double doors and entered the main living room and dining area. Before him were the stairs to the lower deck and main cabins. He took them two at a time, eager to get things ready.

A short time later, he'd finished the trap and left the boat. He hit the lock button to the Jag and grinned wide as the luxury car's lights flashed off and on, welcoming him. He slid behind the wheel and started the engine.

He glanced at his watch before backing out of the space. It read nine twenty five as the last of the faint light faded to dark. He glanced up at the sky, now an angry swirl of clouds, threatening rain. He hoped it held off until they were way out in the ocean.

He knew the cop bars in town, so he drove around, until he spotted Lana's yellow Corvette, parked in the lot of a real dive called the Blue Stingray. An old beat up Stingray sign, with faded blue paint, welcomed those who walked in through the doorway.

The disguise he wore was his best yet. Hell, he could have been Lana's less endowed twin sister. He straightened his short skirt and walked confidently in the 5 inch heels over to the bar. He tossed his long red hair as he sat down on a bar stool in true lady like fashion.

His ice blue eyes scanned the dark bar until he found his marks. Easy prey, the two losers would be so lost in each other's eyes. From his purse he pulled out two small pills, one blue and one white and cupped them in his hands.

He waited until Mike nodded for two more refills, then followed the waitress over to the bar. The bar tender filled the order, of a beer for Mike and a girlie strawberry daiquiri, for soon to be, 'the late' Ms. Lana Turner.

As the waitress lifted her tray with the two drinks on it, he accidently stumbled in front of her. He grabbed the bar to "prevent himself" from falling.

Naturally the waitress set the tray down right in front of him, to make sure he was ok. Expertly he dropped the two pills, one in each glass, as he made a big show of righting himself. He smiled at the waitress and thanked her profusely for saving his life, all the while watching the pills dissolve quickly in the drinks.

"First day in these new heels," he said, in an obviously too high voice.

The waitress didn't notice, not with all the noise in the bar. She smiled and nodded as she looked down at his 5 inch heels.

"Well be careful you don't break your neck in those spanking hot pumps, sista." She winked and walked away, carrying the tray high and still, so as not to spill the drinks.

He quickly walked down the narrow hall and waited just outside the ladies room. Lana's special little pill was designed to make her feel like she was going to puke, while Mike's was a guarantee knock out. Lana's of course would kick in first and dumb ass Mike won't know what hit him, a short time later.

At the end of the long dark hall was a door with a bright red exit sign glowing over top of it. Perfect. Footsteps sounded and he eased himself further into the shadows. He smiled as one Lana Turner rounded the bend, grabbing her stomach. He stepped out and put his arm around her large frame. Even with the heels on, the Amazon red head towered over him.

"Easy honey, you look like you are about to be sick. The bathroom is out of order, but I'll help you get outside so you can get that out of your stomach."

Lana nodded gratefully as she let the woman guide her out through the exit door.

The pill was a two parter and as the second part kicked in, Lana became more and more disoriented. In her eyes he saw that she knew something was horribly wrong, but was helpless to fight it or him. He guided the now drunk appearing woman to his waiting Jag and opened the passenger door. "Watch your head Lana. I best get you home sis, to sleep it off," he said with a giggle as two men passed by, ogling the twin red heads.

Simpletons! He slammed the door shut and went around to the driver's door. Lana was mumbling and attempting to open her door with slow ineffectual movements.

He reached over and pulled the seatbelt across her voluptuous chest and secured her in the seat. "Now, now Lana I won't want you to fall out." His laugh pierced the air as he put the car in reverse and backed out.

So easy. So very, very easy. He floored the car and headed back to the boat. Yes, Swan Dive was a perfect name.

# CHAPTER EIGHTEEN

Kendall nearly puked, as she stared at the once lovely blonde singer, dangling from the beam, with her name carved deep into her flat belly. "Oh my gosh, I think I'm gonna be sick."

She ran her fingers through her layered blonde hair and looked over at Bobbie and CJ who were both white as ghosts.

Kipp exhaled sharply. "He's long gone from here."

Agent Crane nodded. "Yes, the police found foot prints leading to where a motorcycle of some kind must have been hidden. Tracks show he headed due north."

"Well that's helpful," Jerry said sarcastically.

"Easy fellas, we are all doing the best we can." Oliver wrapped his arm across Jerry's shoulders. "You ok hoss?"

"No, I'm not ok. This psychopath has been fucking with us long enough. It is time to end it!" Jerry walked over to where the girls stood.

Oliver shrugged. "Just trying to help."

Andy smiled at him. "We know that Oliver. Jerry knows that too, he's just too macho to admit it."

Joe flipped on his small mag light and squatted down on the dirt floor. "Take a look at this."

Oliver, Debbie, Kipp and Bert squatted down beside him.

"What the hell?" Oliver stood up and motioned for the CSI team to come over. He pointed down. "Can you secure that in a way we can read it?"

The small brunette nodded. "Sure can. Give me a minute and I'll get the stuff."

A short time later, a business card, bearing the name Supreme Yachts, was inside a clear evidence bag and being studied by nearly everyone on the team.

"He's got another boat." Jerry slapped his hand down on an old wooden tack box.

"Get the owner on the phone now!" Kipp shook his head. "We are gonna nail this bastard, tonight."

Debbie Crane motioned for Kendall, CJ and Bobbie to split from the rest of the group and follow her to an unoccupied corner.

She looked each woman in the eyes. "I have to be honest, I've never been comfortable with other females. You know competition and I guess deep down I've always felt a little less than them. So what I'm about to do is a big step for me and probably a fire able offense, but seeing you Kendall and hearing all you've been through, I'm going to take that chance.

Kendall waited for her to go on as did the others. Crane hesitated until Bobbie reached over and squeezed her arm. "We don't bite, ya know."

Debbie Crane smiled for the first time in a long time, while on the job. "No, huh."

"Well, only in certain situations," CJ said with a wink.

"Go on Debbie, please." Kendall looked directly at the agent and for the first time in a long time felt emotionally and mentally strong enough to handle whatever came out of her mouth.

"I believe I know where his new boat is and I'm going to give you a head start from the boys." She handed Bobbie keys and a hand written address. "I've been sniffing around for the last few days for large amounts of money being paid in cash. A boat called Swan Dive was recently purchased from this address. I'm betting it was him. Now I might be wrong, but my intuition is telling me I'm not. Your choice, to go with it or stay here."

"So, what are you ladies talking about?" Jerry eased his way into the circle of women.

"You of course," said Kendall.

"Good, someone is getting her spunk back. I like it!" He punched her lightly on her upper arm.

"Actually Kendall isn't feeling so hot. Debbie offered to let us use her truck to take her back to the hotel."

Kipp approached the group. "I think that is a great idea. She's been through too much today. We can take it from here. Keep your cell phones on in case we need you."

The women nodded, nearly as one and walked out to the waiting FBI black SUV. Bobbie hit the lock buttons then got behind the wheel. Kendall took shot gun and CJ eased into the back seat.

"You think she's setting us up? Bobbie looked at Kendall and then CJ.

"Could be. I've heard a ton of grumbling about her from our people and the other FBI agents and cops. Not sure we should trust her," Kendall said.

"What if she is telling us the truth?" CJ leaned forward between the bucket seats. "You deserve to finish him off. We all do and out there in the big blue ocean the only ones who will know are us and the fishes."

A knock sounded on the window, startling the women. Kendall hit the button and lowered her window to find Andy, CJ's husband, standing there.

"Is CJ with you?"

"U'm." Kendall looked at Bobbie.

CJ opened the back door and got out. "What is it my handsome prince? We are just taking Kendall to the hotel."

Andy looked her up and down and then to Kendall and Bobbie. "I'd really appreciate it if you would stay here and help us with the investigation. We could really use the insight of a female."

Kendall sighed. "Really Andy, isn't that laying it on a little thick?"

He shook his head. "Just speaking the truth ladies."

CJ looked to Kendall and Bobbie for direction.

"Go ahead and stay CJ. We'll be ok going to the hotel, but keep your phone on and close in case we need you." Bobbie looked her directly in the eyes.

"I don't see why I'm needed, especially with the fact you have Agent Crane to lend a females perspective." CJ stood her ground.

"Have you spoken to her? It is like trying to melt ice off of an iceberg to get any type of insight or help from her. We need you CJ and I'd appreciate you respecting me, not as your husband, but as a member of Midnight Riders."

Clearly Andy won as CJ slunk away with a look back at her friends. She tapped the phone attached to her hip and gave them a thumbs up.

"Guess we are on our own," said Bobbie.

"Couldn't think of anyone I'd want beside me more, when this asshole goes down, than you." Kendall squeezed Bobbie's hand.

They drove away, each silently lost in their thoughts of what was to come.

# CHAPTER NINETEEN

He parked the Jag, practically on top of the dock. Swan Dive loomed over the car, big and white and soon to be deadly. He pulled off the red wig and threw it on the passenger side floor. His fake jewelry and high heels followed.

He tapped the rich leather wheel and ran his fingers over the plush seats for the last time. He was going to miss this car, but with his money, he'd have a brand new one, on the Island of his choice.

Lana moaned in the back seat as the drugs started to lose their grip. Her hand slowly reached up, grabbing for anything to hold onto.

Gail got out of the car, still in his short skirt and top and practically ripped the back door off its hinges.  In his right hand he held a charged tazer.

Through bleary eyes Lana looked up at him. He smiled, revealing near perfect white teeth. "Let's go sweet heart. Your yacht awaits." He yanked on her once pretty feminine blouse.

Lana responded slowly, still under the influence of his Mickey. She slid her

feet out the door, intending to kick him
to hell and back. Much to her dismay
her legs kicked out weakly, not even
reaching his knees. "Who are you?" she
said, speech slurred and soft.

"You'll learn that soon enough. Now
get the hell out of the car or I'm going to
hit you with this tazer so hard, I'll have
to drag your unconscious body on to the
boat." Damn, he hoped not. She was way
bigger than him, both in height and
weight. He smiled as her feet hit the
pavement.

Lana looked around the area, trying
to get her bearings as to where she was.
She lowered her hand grabbing for a cell
phone, that was no longer there.

"Looking for this?" Gail wiggled the
pink phone in front of her, then threw it
as hard as he could into the bay. It
landed with a small splash and sunk to
the bottom like a rock. "Now get up."

Lana blinked several times, then
reached up and took hold of the car's
window and hoisted her body into a semi
-standing position. "Why are you doing
this to me? Did I arrest you before?"

"Shut the fuck up bitch and start
moving or so help me I will tazer your
ass and kick your unconscious body
into the bay. By the time they find you,

the fish will have feasted on you, just like Kay Hunter." He motioned with the tazer to go towards the white boat.

Her mind said no, but her legs complied with his wishes. Holding onto the car, she inched her way towards the boat. As she reached the end of the hood, she stared to place her hands down, for balance and stumbled and fell head first onto the wooden dock. Splinters filled her hands as she screamed out in pain.

He hit her with the tazer before another scream left her mouth, knocking her unconscious. "Just great, now how am I going to get this cow up onto the ship?" A thought hit him and he raced up the dock and onto the boat.

From the rear compartments he pulled out a large blanket that he used to cover himself, when the sun got too hot. Quickly he hurried back to the limp girl and rolled her onto the blanket. He wasn't a big man, but thanks to a strict workout regimen, he was able to drag her dead weight down the dock. Still, it took nearly twenty five minutes, to drag her up and onto the boat's tail. He pushed her against the wall and closed the small lower doors.

He leaned against the ships sleek wall and rested. This bitch had caused him enough grief to last him a life time. From his pocket he pulled a capped syringe and jabbed it into Lana's thigh. "That should keep you compliant until we are well out to sea."

Over head lightening cracked, filling the sky with an eerie flash. He jumped, startled by the thunder that followed so quickly. The storm was right over head. He had to move fast.

He leaped over the small doors and ran back to the Jag. Thrusting the keys in the ignition he started the car and backed it away from the dock. A short distance away, a clear shot into the bay waited, for what he was about to do. Throwing the car in park, he left it to go pick up a huge rock sitting beside the dock. He got behind the wheel and released the car into neutral.

He then got out and put the rock on the gas pedal, while still keeping his foot on the brake. The beautiful car's new engine screamed with power as he simultaneously released the brake and threw the car into drive. It took off down the cause way and shot into the bay at a good forty miles per hour. He saluted the car then looked up at the stern of the boat. "Yes, Swan Dive is definitely a good name."

Another flash of lightening and crack of thunder brought his mind back to the job at hand. Quickly he cast off and raced up to the wheel house. He started the engine and expertly thrusted the power, until the boat was away from the dock and moving out to sea.

The waves grew rougher with each passing second as the ship headed to her doom out in the deep blue ocean.

## CHAPTER TWENTY

"Un fucking believable!" Kipp hung up his cell and turned to the group, now staring at him. "That was Deputy Torres giving me a courtesy call. They just picked up Mike Garcia from a local bar and he's doped up good."

"Are you friggen kidding me! We need this like we need a hole in the head with all that is going on!" Jerry kicked the floor with his cowboy boot.

"There's more and I'm glad Kendall isn't here to hear it," Kipp said angrily.

"Let me guess, the big red headed bitch is doped up with him," said CJ

"Worse, she's missing. The waitress says they both started acting strange after she served them their last drinks. Lana got up, appearing sick to her stomach and Mike pretty much passed out at the table. Last she saw of Lana was her heading off to the bathroom and her sister helping her." Kipp shook his head.

"Only problem is she doesn't have a sister, right?" said Andy.

Agent Crane looked at Kipp. "CJ and I can handle this scene. Why don't the rest of you figure out how to deal with Garcia and teaming up with local PD and FBI to find Deputy Turner?"

With new found respect, Kipp nodded at Debbie Crane. "Sounds like a plan. Now who wants to go get Garcia?"

Silence went around the group as no one looked up to meet Kipp's eyes.

"Then I have no choice. Andy, Bert and Joe I want you to head down and see what is up with Mike. Jerry and I will head down to the command post for the search and see what we can find out." He pointed to CJ. "You call Bobbie and Kendall and fill them in on what is going on."

"Will do boss," said CJ.

The teams dispersed leaving CJ with Debbie Crane.

"You better not be setting my friends up Agent Crane. If you are, you will wish you were dead by the time The Midnight Riders get through with you."

"Look, I know we just met and I have the worst reputation in the entire FBI, but after seeing how well you all work together and really care about each other, I've realized I want that far more than any FBI promotion. I promise, I did not set your friends up."

"Can you get hold of another boat?" CJ asked, as she flipped open her phone and dialed Bobbie's number.

"My family has a pretty large yacht docked near the speed boat I lent Bobbie and Kendall. Why?"

"Because you are going to turn this investigation over to someone else and we are going to go help my friends." CJ heard Bobbie say hello. It was difficult to hear with wind and thunder in the back ground.

"We are just heading out now. There is a hell of a storm coming in, but we do have a visual on Swan Dive and are following."

CJ filled them in on Mike and the fact Lana had disappeared. "Crane and I are on the way to support you. Be safe." She hit off and turned to Crane. "Now let's go find us a ride and get the hell out there."

# CHAPTER TWENTY-ONE

He let the big boat drift, even though the seas were high. He had to get his prize down stairs and secured to the bed before she woke up.

The boat tossed and turned, rocked up and down and he grabbed onto anything stationary to keep from falling down as he made his way outside and looked down at the lower deck.

Lana lay face down, with water crashing over her, then draining off the side of the boat. He looked down, weighing his options on how to move the soon to be dead cow. Hell, she weighed that much. He looked up and saw a pulley system, designed to hoist large fish aboard. Turning he made his way down the unsteady stairs and into the master cabin where he grabbed two thick chains.

The wind hit him hard when he exited the living room doors and walked outside again. Rain pelted him in the face and stung his eyes as he lowered himself down next to Lana. Several minutes later, his hands nearly frozen from the cold sea, he had Lana hog tied with the chains and attached to the hoist.

He climbed back up and crawled over to the hoist. Turning it on, he hit the up button and slowly Lana's unconscious body crept top ward. When she reached the upper deck, he stood up and grabbed onto her, swinging the hoist over the top railing. Shielding his eyes from the pounding rain, he hit down and Lana glided to the deck.

Quickly he released the chains, then rolled Lana, once again, onto the blanket and heaved her body inside. As he neared the double doors he slipped on the deck and crashed head first into a deck chair. A deep laceration spewed blood from his forehead filling his eyes so he couldn't see.

"Ahhhhhhhhhhhhh!" He screamed out at the top of his lungs and kicked at Lana, while wiping the blood from his sight. "Fucking storm is going to wreck it for me!"

With a last yank of the blanket, Lana landed inside and he shut the double glass doors behind her, sealing out the storm's wrath, but not the roll and pitch of the boat.

It tossed him to the floor, but this time he grabbed onto the couch instead of smacking his head on the marble tile. He sat up and stayed seated as he dragged himself across the floor and grabbed onto the blanket once again. It took nearly all his strength to get Lana to the tip of the stairs, so he edged behind her, braced his back against the wall and then pushed her off the lip with his feet and leg strength.

She tumbled down the stairs, like a rag doll, and landed with a thud on the carpet below. He took one step at a time on his butt. When he reached the bottom he stood up and held onto the wooden railing attached to the wall, for rich bitches to keep their balance, in situations just like this.

He had no fear the boat would sink as she was big and top rated for storms. What he feared, was getting killed by the ship tossing him into or down something during the storm. He opened the master cabin's door and put a bench against it to keep it open. Once again and for the final time he grabbed the blanket and heaved Lana into the room and then up onto the big bed.

Exhausted, he slid down onto the floor and rested his body against the side of the bed. Above him he heard Lana moan. "Damn it bitch, can't you give me a second to rest?"

He jerked himself up and balanced using the strength of his muscled legs and strong core. Hell, he'd only done it to seduce whores, but tonight it was coming in mighty handy in other ways. Easily he balanced himself as he secured Lana spread eagle to the bed with the chains he'd secured to the wall earlier in the day.

He slapped her. "Wake up Lana darling."

Lana's eyes slowly opened, like you see in a movie, after great sex. He laughed when they went wide with terror as she focused her sight on him.

"I'm glad you are a wake. I won't want you to miss one thing I'm going to do to you." From his bag he pulled out scissors and moved them back and forth before her eyes. Suddenly the ship rolled sharply to the left and the scissors jabbed down stabbing Lana in her arm. "Whoopsie," he said, then cackled in a high pitch sound.

"Ahhh!" Tears, like the storm's water outside the cabin, dripped from Lana's blood shot eyes. "Please don't hurt me. I've never done anything to you."

He leaned forward, his face inches from hers. "You still don't remember me, do you?"

She studied him. "Wait you're the NCIS agent I met on the beach." She pulled against the chains, panic in her eyes. "Now I remember. You're Mike Kendall."

"Wow, you really are a stupid cow aren't you?" He waited until he saw the light bulb go on in her head. "Let me introduce myself." He dragged the tip of the scissors across her legs breaking the skin in long, weeping lines. "My name is Chris Hawthorne and I'm your worst nightmare come true, whore."

He picked up the scissors and cut off all her clothes while she screamed at the top of her big lungs and flailed against the chains holding her captive. She wrenched to the right and the scissors dove into the fat of her upper leg. Blood flowed slowly from the deep cut.

He leaned forward again, holding himself still with his legs and core. "I heard you were into kinky sex. Like a little pain, do you?"

He picked up her long trade mark red hair and started hacking away. It fell on her face, body and the floor, until all that was left of her once beautiful mane, was uneven, short jagged clumps of hair. "I'm sure Mike will like you any way. Not!"

Next he took out nipple clamps and screwed them onto Lana's until, she screamed with pain. He yanked on the chain that attached the two, drawing blood as they scrapped along her flesh, but still stayed attached.

"Isn't this fun?" He reached into his dark bag of tricks and pulled out a big black dildo which he shoved up her ass. Blood shot out as it ripped her sensitive inside.

Through pain and free flowing tears, she watched as he lowered his zipper and dropped his pants to the floor. A grotesque smile covered his handsome face as he hopped onto the bed then straddled her. He leaned down kissing her, pushing her mouth open with his teeth and tongue. Next came his cock as he rammed it in and out of her mouth. She bit down hard.

He screamed, pulling his dick out. The last thing she saw was his fist thundering towards her face.

# CHAPTER TWENTY-TWO

Andy, Joe and Bert walked solemnly into the police station. Faces grim and determined they approached the desk jockey.

"Good evening, we are here to see Mike Garcia," said Andy.

The dispatcher reached over and hit the lock button. "Come on in through the door on the right."

The three men walked single file through the door and into a small waiting area.

"Please have a seat. Deputy Torres will be with you shortly," said the young female dispatcher.

They all sat down on the hard orange- plastic chairs, not speaking. Each looked up as the door opened and in walked Deputy Torres with Mike trailing behind him.

"Sit down Mike," said Torres, pointing to a chair across from the other three men. "Mike has an interesting story to tell and one we are in the process of collaborating. If he's right, Deputy Lana Turner is in deep trouble."

Mike looked at his former friends and partners through blood shot eyes. "Look, I know you can't stand the sight of me right now and I don't blame you. I'm asking you for help anyway. Will you help me?"

Andy looked to Joe and Bert who both nodded.

"Let's hear what you have to say Mike and then we'll decide if it warrants our help," said Andy.

"Thank you." Mike inhaled deeply before continuing. The Mickey still in his system made him slow and clouded his mind. "I know Deputy Torres filled you in on Lana and I both being slipped an unknown drug or drugs. What he didn't tell you is that as soon as I started to feel weird I got up to follow Lana. I knew something was wrong. I saw her being led outside by a shorter red head. I was able to make it out the exit door, before I went down. I got a partial plate of the car she got into. They are running combinations now for anything suspicious or that stands out." Mike leaned back in the chair and shut his eyes. "Man, the room is spinning."

"Detective Torres we have the print out for you." The dispatcher handed the burly cop a computer print out. "Nothing stands out to me, but it might to you."

Torres handed the print out to Andy and the guys gathered around it.

Scanning the sheet Joe stopped at one name. "Holy hell, do you see what I see?"

"Shit!" Bert stood up. "We need to run the name Mike Kendall for an address, car or boat insurance  or registrations. Can you do that?"

"Absolutely. Just give me the correct spelling and I'll get them on it." Torres wrote the correct spelling down on a piece of paper and rushed it into dispatch.

Mike's head lolled back, against the wall as his breathing deepened.

"I think he needs to get to the ED. Let's have them call for a rig and get him to medical help and out of our hair," said Andy.

The others nodded. Bert knocked on the dispatch door, just as Torres pushed it open.  He handed Bert a paper with two addressed on it. One to an apartment and the other to a brand new boat.

"Great job! What is the plan deputy?" said Bert.

"Right now our units are heading for both places to check them out. I'll have an update in about ten minutes and based on that I think we will be able to come up with a game plan."

Joe pointed to Mike. "He needs to get to a hospital. Can you call a rig, please."

Torres rolled his eyes then stepped back into dispatch. A few minutes later he reappeared. "The rigs on the way. One of my deputies will wait with Mike until it arrives. We are going to the boat slip, which they just found empty. There are tire tracks leading into the water and they believe a car is submerged."

Andy inhaled sharply. "Let's go!" He pulled out his phone and dialed Kipp's number.

The four men walked out of the waiting room without a look back at the now snoring Mike Garcia.

# CHAPTER TWENTY-THREE

The black SUV idled in the yacht club parking lot. Inside Kendall and Bobbie finalized their plan of attack.

"Are you sure you are strong enough to handle this Kendall?"

"I've been to hell and back and nothing is going to stop me from finishing the job. I'm ready," said Kendall. She opened the door and got out into a light mist falling. From the back hatch, she pulled out a brown water proof gym bag, filled with weapons of every shape and size.

Together the women walked down the dock until they found the sleek, bright red, speed boat, matching Debbie Crane's description. Kendall stepped aboard first with Bobbie close behind.

"Here goes nothing," said Bobbie as she slipped the key in to the starter. It fit like a glove and the powerful engine sprung to life with a quick turn.

Kendall went to the long bow and released the tie while Bobbie did the same to the stern.

"Ready partner?" Bobbie said loudly, over the engine's noise.

"Hell yeah!" Kendall grabbed hold of the window frame and stood watching out over the bow. "Looks like a storm is moving in. I hope this boat can handle it."

Bobbie pointed to a small cargo hold. "Better see if there are wet suits and life vests like Debbie said there'd be."

Kendall inched forward, balancing herself each time the boat struck a wave. She knelt down and opened a small hatch door. Inside there were several wet suits of various sizes and a bunch of life vests. She pulled two suits out that looked their sizes as well as two life vests.

Bobbie cut the engine to idle and slipped on the wet suit and vest while Kendall did the same. Once ready, the boat shot through the waves, heading towards whatever awaited them.

Lightning flashed across the sky as the wind and rain picked up and the sleek boat fought its way out of the bay and into the ocean.

# CHAPTER TWENTY-FOUR

She woke up naked and handcuffed to a chain, that was secured by a bolt, to the cabin wall. Water lapped at her feet, pouring in to the small room. Pure fear filled her.

This was it, there was no way out of this one. She was fucked!

Thick clumps of her long, hacked off red hair floated past her in the rising water. She now looked like Pink only not so pretty.

"Help me! Help me!" she screamed, until her throat went raw with pain.

The bastard had done things to her, her mind, her body, more vile than she'd ever imagined. Her spirit lay shattered, deep inside her broken body.

Yanking hard against the chain and handcuffs, she fought to stay alive as the water swirled deep and deeper covering her.

The water licked at her chin. She raised her face nose to the ceiling. She inhaled one last desperate breath as the water rose over her mouth and nose. Seconds later she was underwater, waiting to die.

# CHAPTER TWENTY-FIVE

Bobbie cut the speed boat's engine, letting the boat drift in the every roughening sea. A strong storm, clearly on the horizon was headed their way.

They had to move fast, strike the sick piece of shit while, he least expected it. A few hundred yards to the west, Kay Hunter's yacht, lights twinkling in the darkness, bobbed up and down, handling the high seas like child's play.

Gas thought he'd broken her, but he was dead wrong. Nothing was going to stop her from ending this tonight. Nothing!

What little light had been filtering through the rain now descended below the horizon, pitching them into complete darkness.

"Let me go, Kendall. You are just getting your mental and physical strength back. You are no match for him." Bobbie held steady on the wheel as the boat rocked back and forth in the roughening seas.

She slipped on the scuba pack, wiggled her feet into the flippers then picked her mask and snorkel. "If I don't do this Bobbie I am as good as dead. I have to end this. I have to be the one to face him. He took my trust, my body and part of my soul and I want them back!"

Bobbie nodded. "I understand. You are my best friend and I don't know what I'd do without you."

Kendall reached over and squeezed Bobbie's upper arm. "I won't let you down." She tapped the water proof walkie talkie on her belt and the GPS, set to hone in on the speed boat. "I've got what I need. Let's get this done."

She sat on the speed boat's side and dropped backwards into the sea. The freezing water, deep and dark rushed up to meet her. Unbelievable cold, of the deep ocean, reached in through her wet suit, tickling away the warmth it provided.

Pulling straps over the black wet suit hood she pulled the mask down, covering her face. Using the flippers she kept steady in the water, until she acclimated.

Reaching down, she touched the knife in her boot and the seal team issued gun, secured to her belt. Courage filled her as she got ready to eliminate her mark.

Pushing the on button, the GPS dial lit up, revealing the direction she faced and where the speed boat was. In the deep, dark water it was easy to get turned around and off course. She kicked her feet, angling around, until the coordinates matched where the yacht sat.

She dove under the water, kicking her flippers and propelling her body towards the target. She estimated it would take about 20 minutes to swim to the yacht. Her tank was good for an hour, so she had plenty of time and life saving air to spare.

Despite the roaring storm raging above, the water under the surface, was calm and easy to move through. Fifteen minutes later, she spotted the yachts white hull, a dull gray color in the dark ocean.

Rage coiled inside her, ready to spring for the kill as soon as she saw her prey. She touched the hull with her gloved hand and felt around in the dark, until she was near the back of the large boat.

It suddenly hit her that the propellers weren't moving, not even a slow idle to keep the yacht steady in the high sea. The huge boat drifted through the ocean as if no one controlled her helm.

She gripped the lower rear deck pad and launched herself up onto it. Noiselessly she held onto the rails and slowly climbed up to the deck.

A deafening boom sounded, shaking the boat wildly. The jarring ripped her hand off the rail and tossed her onto the deck. She lay there momentarily stunned, until she heard the sound of a small engine starting. Edging herself up, she held onto the railing and watched a small emergency life boat shoot away from the bow and quickly distanced itself from the yacht, now obviously taking on water.

"Mother fucker!" she yelled through the raging storm. Now what? Then she heard it, faintly. A sound drifted through the air, carried by the storm. Someone was still on board! Pulling out the walkie talkie she radioed Bobbie, telling her of the escaping life boat.

She glanced at the yacht's bow, watching as it rapidly started taking on water, sinking below the surface. Fear shot through her. If she went below, she could easily get trapped and sink with the ship. If she didn't she'd, have to  live with the guilt of letting her die.

She knew immediately who was yelling for help and part of her wanted to let the bitch drown. Then she'd have Mike back and everything would be normal.

"Damn it!" She shook her head and smacked her hand against the deck wall, grabbed the sliding deck door's handle and pulled.

She'd memorized the yachts blueprint, knew it by heart. Inside on the main party deck, the water was nowhere to be seen. Balancing, using her hands to grab onto the wall, chairs, anything to hold her steady, she walked gingerly through the bar/living room and peered down the stairs leading to the cabins.

Water sloshed against the bottom step. Reaching down she pulled off her flippers and left them next to the bar. Bare footed she fought to stay upright as she negotiated the stairs. The intense storm was now tossing the big boat around, with no engines to steady her.

The yells for help had stopped seconds ago so with no time to waste, she threw her body against the farthest door, which she knew was the master cabin. The hinges broke and water poured into the room as the door crashed down.

Pulling the flashlight from her belt, she flipped it on as she waded through the now, waist deep water. Shining it around the room, she searched for the trapped woman.

"Lana!" she yelled at the top of her lungs, fighting against the noise of the charging water and storm. When no answer came she turned away, ready to go check the other cabins. She gasped as something grabbed her leg.

"Holy shit!" She looked down to see a hand, with a handcuff around the wrist, latched onto her leg.

Quickly she put in her mouth piece, pulled the mask over her face and sunk beneath the chest height water. The water proof flashlight cut through the darkness and landed on the panicked face of Deputy Lana Turner.

Swimming over to the handcuffed woman, so obviously running out of air, she pulled the bolt cutter from her belt and swiftly cut the handcuff's chain. Lana floated free, too weak to help Kendall get her head above water.

Reaching down Kendall wrapped her arms underneath Lana's and despite the fact the redhead far out weighing her, she heaved her to the surface. Lana inhaled a shallow breath.

"Come on Lana! You've got to take a breath!" Kendall did a sternal rub, which made Lana pop her head up and open her eyes.

Holding Lana's head above the water, Kendall pulled her over to the cabin door, nearly covered over with ice cold ocean. Removing the mouth piece, she pushed it through Lana's blue lips. "Take a breath Lana! Now!"

The yacht lurched further into the sea. It was now or never if they were going to make it out. With a yank, Kendall got Lana and herself through the door and surfaced in the hallway, now filled waist deep with swirling water.

"Now how the hell am I going to get you up the stairs?" She looked down at the woman, whose head she was holding, just above the water. Lana, the one woman who stood between her and Mike and she held her life literally in her hands. Shaking away her angry thoughts, she maneuvered behind Lana and once again put her arms underneath the sluggish woman and edged her closer to the stairs.

"Come on Lana! Open your eyes and get in the game. You out weigh me by a ton, so help me or you are going down with the ship!"

Lana nodded and slowly moved her legs as Kendall sat her butt on the first step and hoisted the other woman up, step by step. Reaching the main level, she gave one last pull and Lana lay supine on the floor.

Kendall looked around the room for flotation devices and spotted two life jackets, on the far wall. She grabbed them and threw them to Lana. "Put them on. There is no way I'm going to be able to get you off this boat and over to mine, if it's even still afloat, if you don't help me."

Shaking the fog from her brain, Lana picked up the life jackets and slowly pushed one arm through the opening. Water lapped at the top of the stairs as she swung the jacket around her back and tried to find the other arm hole.

Kendall watched from across the room with one part of her wanting to leave the deputy and the other knowing, she'd never be able to live with herself if she did.

"Oh hell!" Kendall braced herself on the table, then grabbed onto a bolted in chair as she made her way back across the room. The sea was churning mad and spitting up into the main deck. Kendall bent down, bracing her legs shoulder width apart and helped Lana put on the first one in the back and then strapped the other one across her large naked breasts.

"Am I dead?" Lana's big, green eyes gazed up at Kendall.

Kendall snorted. "Hardly honey, cause there is no way in hell, I'm going to be stuck with you in the afterlife. Come on, we have to get off this sinking tub. Crawl if you have to, but get going or I'm leaving you here!"

Lana nodded as she slowly got onto her knees and started to crawl behind Kendall. They went through the double sliders as rain, wind and ocean pelted the two women with horrific force.

Kendall grabbed onto Lana's vest and helped her over to the edge of the boat. The yacht rose up and down as each giant wave hit her.

Lana looked up at Kendall. "Thank you for saving me. I'm so sorry. So very, very sorry for hurting you."

Kendall nodded. "We can talk later if we manage to get off of this boat and make it alive through this storm."

The sea tossed the two women back and forth as they slowly managed to reach the vessels stern, now starting to rise into the air. They only had moments to spare before it disappeared to a watery grave and took them with her.

"We're gonna have to jump Lana. Put your hands on the rail and I'll help you over."

As a team the two women maneuvered to the railing and stood up, holding onto it's cold metal. Kendall looked at Lana.

"She's going down fast. Get your feet and butt over the rail and let go. I'll be right behind you." Kendall bent down and pulled on the flippers she'd carried out with her.

Gail force winds belted Lana's weakening body as she used her upper body to pull her up and over the railing. She nosed dived off it and fell head first into the violent waves.

Kendall dropped in right behind her and desperately searched for the stricken woman. "Lana!" she yelled.

To her right she spotted the orange life vest pop up to the surface with Lana still snug inside. Kendall kicked the flippers with all her might and swam to Lana. She grabbed onto the life vest and started swimming away from the yacht, now in her death spiral. If they stayed close the suction would pull them under. When the two women were about a hundred yards away the yacht gave a death roar and everything inside her let loose, as she slipped beneath the waves.

Alone now in the storm, the two women clung together. Kendall looked down at her GPS watch and activated it. The screen searched for the speed boat's signal as huge waves carried the two women up and down like they were on a merry go round - one you could drown on.

"Please God, please let Bobbie and the boat still be there." Kendall thought of Bobbie, out there in the storm and she prayed she was safe. Their only hope was Bobbie and the speedboat. Without both of them they were good as dead. A red dot appeared on the screen. "Thank you! Oh thank you!!"

She held the GPS in front of Lana, who took in a mouth full of sea water, gasping, choking and retching, all at the same time.

Kendall grimaced at the other woman's distress. "Hang in there Lana. I know you're hurt and freezing cold, but we can do this! We have a chance now with my boat still floating out there. It looks to be only a short distance from where we are. Do you think you can make it if I help you?"

Lana nodded as new resolve shown in her face. "That bastard isn't taking me down. Let's go."

Together they fought through the waves and as they got closer to the signal area Kendall turned on her light. It shone through the storm and landed on the most beautiful sight of Bobbie, holding the boat steady, in the violent sea. Bobbie waved as the red speed boat crested each wave then crashed to the sea below. Timing would be everything.

"Okay, Lana, when the boat crests the wave grab on and get in. I'll help you and so will Bobbie."

Kendall and Lana swam into the same wave the boat was cresting and Bobbie yanked Lana onto the boat with Kendall pushing from behind.

The now short haired red head flopped into the boat, landing with a thud, just as the speed boat dropped out of the wave. Kendall let go and fell alongside. With the next wave, she grabbed the boat's side and Bobbie helped her climb aboard.

From the bench seat Bobbie pulled out two blankets and wrapped them around Lana's naked body. "I'm so thankful you are ok Kendall. I was worried beyond tears." She reached out and hugged her friend as they balanced on the slippery deck. The wind and rain picked up, pelting the three women.

The exhausted women huddled together on the boat's floor, holding a yellow water proof tarp over themselves, as rain, wind and waved crashed onto them. How the boat was staying afloat was a mystery and Kendall knew someone up above was watching over them, for sure.

The storm lasted another half hour, then suddenly blew away and the sky cleared. The night sky filled with beautiful twinkling stars, a full moon and hearts full of revenge.

"So where did you find her?" Bobbie said, pointing to a shivering Lana.

The once long haired beauty sat up slowly. "She saved my life. Gail Gas drugged and kidnapped me. I'd be dead without you Kendall." She reached over and hugged Kendall. "Thank you for saving my life. I know you hate me and could easily have left me there, but you didn't. Thank you."

Kendall sighed. "I don't hate you, Lana. In all honesty, things have been bad between Mike and I ever since Hawthorne, Gail Gas, or whatever the hell the piece of shit is calling himself, seduced, raped and tortured me."

"I'm so sorry," Lana said softly.

"He also brutalized me while I was helpless." She looked into Lana's knowing eyes.

"I hate him and I want him dead!" Lana spat over the side.

"You and me both." Kendall grabbed onto the captain's chair and slowly stood up on wobbly legs. She eased herself into the chair and said a silent prayer. With any luck they'd find him and end this thing tonight once and for all.

"Get yourselves secured. We have some hunting to do." Bobbie hit the gas and the speed boat took off in the direction the slow moving life boat had headed.

# CHAPTER TWENTY-SIX

Jerry ran his fingers through his light brown hair. "Where the hell are they?"

Kipp bent over the computer at the command post.

Oliver looked up at the huge real time map, covering the far wall of the conference room, they'd been given to use as a command post. He picked up a laser pointer and walked over to the map. "Let's go over what we do know."

Jerry walked over and stood next to him. Kipp picked up a magnetized red x and slapped it over the a dive bar named the Blue Stingray .

"We know Lana and Mike went here and were both drugged," Kipp said.

Oliver turned on the laser and circled the red light around the area of the bar, coming to a stop over the industrial section of the city.

He tapped on an abandoned warehouse near a small inlet. "This is where the bodies of two cops were found, after apparently making a traffic stop. The CSI team found evidence that a vehicle of some kind was recently there, other than the patrol car and based on the tire tracks, it appears to be a late model luxury car, of some kind.

All the men turned as the conference door swung open, hitting the wall with a loud thud. In walked Andy, Joe and Bert.

"The team is here and ready to go!" said Andy. He sure hoped CJ was doing ok with Agent "The Ice Queen" Crane.

Kipp waved them over. "We're running through all we do know so far."

The team surrounded the map as Kipp updated the new arrivals.

"Okay, so where did he take Lana? Andy said.

"The hell with Lana! Where are Kendall and Bobbie? I've been trying to reach them and neither is answering their phones. They are the ones we need to concentrate on, not some Florida slut!" Jerry said angrily.

Heads nodding, the team turned back to the map.

"So what do we know about Kendall and Bobbie's plan?" Kipp looked each member of the team in their eyes.

Andy inhaled sharply. "I know they were talking about finishing him off once and for all. I guess they didn't trust us enough to know anymore than that."

Jerry held up his hands. "I did hear them mention something about boats." He nodded. "Yes, definitely, they were getting boats ready for whatever they were planning."

Oliver scanned the map, his eyes going wide as he saw it. Pointing the red laser forward he stopped it directly over a small inlet of water, close to the warehouse. "This is what we missed! The bastard has a new yacht. Probably stashed a small boat or raft here and took Lana out to the yacht."

Deputy Torres entered the room in a rush. "They found the slip empty, that housed Gas's newest boat and a submerged Jaguar in the inlet, right next to it.

Kipp place a red magnetic x over top of the inlet.

Oliver hung up his phone. "Damn it. They won't launch any boats. The storm is too intense they say to go out now."

Jerry smashed his hand down on the table. "Damn it! Kendall and Bobbie are out there and we have to wait until morning!!"

All eyes turned as the door opened and in walked a bleary eyed Mike

Garcia, fresh from the hospital, with still bleeding IV track marks.

"What the hell are you doing here?" Kipp stepped towards the once esteemed team member.

"You aren't part of this team anymore." Jerry stayed back, glaring at Mike.

The others stood in stoned silence.

"I happen to know where we can get a large fishing boat. I might not have a job with this team, but frankly I don't give a fuck. Follow me." Mike said.

The team hesitated, then followed their former leader out the door bent on finding the women, before it was too late.

# CHAPTER TWENTY-SEVEN

Debbie angled the large boat into the waves and hung on as it drove up and then dropped, like a hot potato. She prayed Kendall and Bobbie were ok and having better luck navigating the storm than she and CJ were. The storm had come on so fast.

The boat's engine struggled to stay going as water crashed over the wheel house compartment. CJ pulled out her phone and dialed for what felt like the hundredth time. "Please answer Kendall."

On the fifth ring she exhaled the breath she'd been holding as Kendall's voice filled her ear.

"Kendall are you ok?"

"I'm ok and so is Bobbie. We almost bought it, but we made it through one of the worst storms I've ever been in. I also have Lana with me. Gas got away. He tried to send Lana to live with the fishes on Hunter's yacht."

"Son of a bitch." CJ looked up as the storm suddenly passed and the ocean calmed. "Thank God the storm is over!"

"It just cleared about twenty minutes ago for us. Where the heck are you?"

"Riding shotgun, on Agent Cranes big -ass boat. We must be pretty close. What are your coordinates?"

CJ read them off to Debbie, who put them in the GPS.

"Head this way and we'll meet up in less than ten minutes." Kendall hung up and turned to Lana. "Do you feel well enough to join us in the hunt?"

Lana stood up on wobbly legs and slowly walked to the passenger seat. She lowered her bruised body gingerly into the seat. "Won't miss it for the world."

Ten minutes later the speed boat was tethered to Debbie's yacht. The women sat together around the plush galley table.

"I saw him take off in the zodiac rescue boat just after the explosion went off. According to my GPS he was headed straight to the gulf of Mexico." Kendall hit the table with her fist.

"So, if the son of a bitch sneaks into Mexico that's it. He's free to start torturing and killing women. Ain't gonna happen on my shift!" Lana stood up quickly, her wobbly legs shaking .

"Whoa, sit down. Last thing we need is for you to fall into the ocean." Bobbie helped Lana lower herself back onto the seat.

"Sorry. I'm just so pissed. He can't do what he did to me... and Kendall and get away with it." Tears dripped from Lana's eyes.

"She's right you know." Kendall looked at Bobbie.

"I know. I'm with you in whatever you decide to do." Bobbie turned to the CJ and Debbie. "What about you guys?"

"I'm in." CJ put her hand out on the table and the others put one of theirs on top of it, one at a time.

"I'm an Agent..." Debbie said not adding her hand.

"We understand Debbie, so in that case this is where we get off." CJ stood and motioned for the three other women to follow her.

Kendall looked down over the railing. "The speed boat is much faster than the zodiac he was in. I'm sure we can catch up to him if we can find him."

Lana wiped her face with the blanket wrapped around her nearly nude body. "Can I have some clothes before we go hunt the mother f'-er?"

Kendall looked back at Debbie. "Do you have any extra clothes on your boat? Lana can't go after the creep naked."

Debbie nodded and hurried down to the main cabins. "I'm pretty sure I saw some of my dad's sweat pants and shirts during my boat check. A short time later she came back with a pair of black sweats and a matching sweat shirt.

Gratefully Lana pulled the sweat shirt over her head and then slipped on the pants. Since they were men's pants, they fit her perfectly and she pulled the warm fabric over her freezing, cold legs, sighing happily. "Thank you Debbie. I think I've died and gone to heaven, these feel so good."

Debbie stood back from the group. "I wish you well. I really do."

The other women smiled back at the by the book FBI agent.

Kendall stepped forward and hugged her. "Thank you for everything Debbie. We have it from here and as far as we are concerned.... "Debbie who?"

Agent Crane smiled and waved as single file the women lowered themselves down onto the red speed boat.

Kendall looked at Lana. "So now that you are decent let's get this show on the road." Kendall sat down in the driver's seat.

Bobbie hopped into the passenger seat and pulled out her gun. The others sat down and did the same. Kendall started the engine and headed west towards the Gulf of Mexico. One way or the other this was ending tonight.

## CHAPTER TWENTY-EIGHT

They caught up to him a little after three a.m.  They watched through night vision goggles as the small zodiac raced along towards Mexico and freedom.

Kendall motioned for Bobbie to get a clear look at him, through the night goggles. They weren't fools and knew he was armed to the hilt.

The first shot rang out, zipping past Kendall, and  finding it's mark, right next to where Lana was sitting. Lana squealed and dropped to her knees, not hit.

"Damn freak, must have night vision too." Kendall turned the wheel hard.

Lana held onto the seat as the boat evaded  rapid fire shots. "Now what are we going to do?

From the left another gunshot sounded finding it's mark in the zodiac's side. Even from the distance they were at, they heard the whoosh of air spewing from the raft.

The women looked up as a huge yacht came into view with Debbie Crane

~at the helm. She waved and gave a thumbs up to the smaller craft.

"No! Damn you fucking cunts!" Gas screamed as he fired his gun wildly at the two boats. None found their mark.

The women idled in their boats well out of range as they watched the zodiac and Gas slowly sink into the sea. The crazed psychopath struggled to get on his scuba gear before he disappeared under the waves.

This area of the gulf, known as the Sigsbee Deep, was the deepest depth, in the whole body of water. Predatory sharks were well known to hunt in the gulf, so you never knew when they'd show up, if the chow bell rang, by say, a body falling into the water.

With miles to go before land even came into sight, there was no way Gas was going to be able to swim it and survive.

Kendall closed the distance between the speed boat and Debbie's yacht. CJ secured the smaller boat and she and Bobbie climbed up the ladder, to join Debbie on board. Separately, each women, sat silently, wrestling with the consequences of letting the serial killer die.

"Let's put some distance between him and us. He could be swimming at us right now." Kendall started the speed boat's engine and Lana cast off.

Two miles later they stopped and idled side by side.

"It will be light in less than four hours and then we can decide what to do." Lana relaxed on the back bench seat of the speed boat.

"We haven't done anything to regret...yet." Kendall looked out over the bow.

An hour later Lana ran her fingers through her jagged short hair. "I'm beginning to have my doubts. I mean I hate him more than life, but I'm no killer."

"Me either," said Bobbie now sitting on the speed boat.

"Same here," said Kendall. She pulled up the marine radio and pressed the button to speak. A hand shot out of the water, grabbing her wrist and pulling her into the water.

Lana and Bobbie screamed as they jumped forward and held onto Kendall, in a tug of war, for her life. Lana motioned for Bobbie to hold on as she reached into Kendall's back pack and pulled out a knife.

Bobbie's hands screamed in agony, clearly not winning the battle as Kendall's head disappeared under the water. "Hurry Lana! I can't hold on!"

Lana, in all her 6 feet of powerful beauty, dove from the opposite side of the boat and disappeared.

In the struggle of her life, Kendall bit Gas in the arm, taking in water and struggling to remain conscious. With eyes open she watched his mouth form into a big smile as air bubbles flitted from her mouth towards the surface.

She was no match for this psychopath. He was evil beyond anything she could have dreamed. He'd once made her feel sexy and alive, but now he held her down, draining the last bit of oxygen from her. Life was leaving and she felt it down to the smallest cells of her body.

Please take care of Bela and my friends God, she silently prayed. She felt numbness traveling up her body as the water claimed her.

His sudden release of her jarred her back awake. She opened her eyes and saw a frown on his face, as blood started flowing, from a pebble sized hole in his right cheek. She pushed off of his body with her legs and sprang to the surface.

She burst through the surface with Lana helping her up by pushing her from below. Lana's head popped up right next to her and she felt herself being pulled into the boat.

"Oh no! Is she ok? Kendall open your eyes!" Bobby said.

Lana knelt down next to Kendall and turned her on her side and pushed on her belly.

Kendall puked up water and inhaled deeply. She rolled onto her back, looking up at the night sky, that was slowly turning to day.

Tears fell from her eyes. "He was smiling as I was dying. Like I was a piece of nothing."

Bobbie hugged her tightly as Lana rubbed her back.

"He won't ever smile again Kendall. That I can promise you." She wrapped her gun in a towel to turn into the brass for review.

"Thank you Lana." She sat up and smiled. "I guess that makes us even." Kendall reached out and took Lana's hand in hers.

Lana nodded. "I'm so sorry..."

Kendall held up her hand. "Someday we can talk, but today let's just pretend we are friends and get the hell back to shore."

"Holy shit!" Bobbie pointed off the starboard side. Gas popped to the surface, a gaping hole in his cheek drained blood into the water. He stayed stark still, aiming a gun directly at Lana's head. The red target light honed in on her right temple, as the night slowly turned to day.

Horror ran up and down their spines as Gail's once handsome face exploded, like a bomb going off. A silver spear gun glittered in Debbie Crane's hands. CJ stood by her side.

Shark fins surfaced in the water, surrounding both boats. Suddenly the water looked like it was boiling as shark after shark descended in a feeding frenzy. Gail Gas's limp body quickly shredded, until nothing remained of the psychopathic serial killer and he was no more.

Kendall shook her head. "That was gross!"

Bobbie hugged herself. "You can say that again."

Lana rocked back on her feet. "That's one body that will never be found."

Kendall reached down and grabbed Lana's gun. The towel fell to the floor. She unloaded it and threw the bullets into the water. Next she looked Bobbie and Lana in the eyes. "Ok?"

Lana nodded.

"Hell yeah!" Bobbie said.

Kendall dropped the gun into the deep ocean and the three of them watched as it sank down to depths no scuba person would ever go.

The three of them hugged.

"Now let's go see how Debbie is doing." Kendall started the boat as Bobbie jumped into her seat and Lana did the same.

Slowly they made their way through the shark's feeding frenzy and over to the yacht. CJ threw down the rope and once again the speed boat was secured to the larger one. They climbed on board.

Lana walked forward immediately and hugged Debbie, who still held the spear gun in her hands. "Thank you for saving my life. I will never forget this." With that she grabbed the spear gun and tossed it off the boat and into the endless sea.

"Wait that's evidence. I killed a man and..."

Kendall patted her back as did the others. "Girlfriend, I didn't see nothin."

"Me either," said Bobbie.

"Nope sun was in my eyes. All I saw were shark fins," said CJ.

For the first time in her life Debbie Crane felt her heart crack wide open. Acceptance, true friendship and a whole new life awaited her. "All for one and one for all," she said loudly.

Kendall started to laugh as did the others.

CJ stretched out her hand and each one of them put their hands on top of hers, this time. "We are free!"

"Now let's get the hell out of here. I'm cold, tired and for the first time in nearly a year I'm going to sleep like a baby." Kendall turned and walked over to the railing. She pointed down to the speed boat. "Care to join me Lana. We have some talking to do."

Lana nodded and followed her over the railing and down to the speed boat.

"Meet you back in port. Follow me," said Debbie Crane as she waved good bye.

Kendall pushed the throttle and the boat picked up speed leaving the gruesome scene and Gail Gas behind like a distant memory.

# CHAPTER TWENTY-NINE

It was early dawn as the team boarded the large fishing vessel and prepared to cast off.

It was Kipp who first heard them. "Wait I hear a boat coming!" He raced to the front of the fishing boat and looked out into the bay.

Kendall came into view driving a red speed boat full tilt with Lana sitting beside her in the passenger seat.

CJ waved and shouted from the large yacht that Kendall had blown by as soon as she'd spied land.

The two boats docked. Kendall and Lana hugged then stepped off onto the dock.

Mike ran towards the women with Jerry at his side. "Lana," he whispered. Relief shone on his handsome face.

Jerry grabbed his arm and stopped him just as he reached the two women. Jerry turned and stared at the man next to him. "You're a real dick, Mike. You know that?"

Mike turned white as he realized he'd said her name out loud, without even acknowledging Kendall was alive. She'd clearly heard him. "Kendall..."

She turned her back on the man she'd once considered the love of her life and started walking down the dock

Within seconds the women were surrounded by their friends.

Lana scanned the group then looked up to find Mike staring at her. Their eyes locked and she discreetly walked away from the group and headed up the boat gangway. Mike met her half way and hugged her to his chest.

"I thought I'd lost you." He kissed the top of her short hair. "Are you ok? Did he hurt you?"

Lana kissed him on his lips then whispered in his ear. "Kendall saved me, so let's be respectful and we can be together later, ok love?"

He nodded and released her from his strong grip. They turned to find the team staring up at them with frowns on their faces. Kipp shook his head then turned his attention back to Kendall.

The hurt in Kendall's eyes were unmistakable. "It's ok guys. I know Mike and I are over and Lana's a good person, once you get to know her."

CJ reached out, hugging her friends, two old and one brand new.

"Let's get out of our wet clothing and get something to eat before the Florida authorities descend.

"That sounds like heaven," said Bobbie. She turned and put her arm around Kendall's shoulders, guiding her away from the heartache standing on the gangway.

"He's a loser girlfriend. You can do better," Bobbie whispered in Kendall's ear.

Debbie opened the back door to an idling MRI black suburban. "In you go. The truck's nice and warm."

Kendall slid in with Bobbie next to her. Her heart was breaking into a million pieces as she watched the man she loved with all her heart put his arm around Lana and escort her to the other truck.

"Don't watch Kendall." CJ pulled the visor down, blocking the view out the front window. "He isn't worth it. That guy hasn't been right for a long time. He's chosen his allegiance to money and now Lana. Let him go."

"How do you let someone go who has been in your life for so long? It should be me next to him in that truck, but it isn't. He's chosen Lana and it's breaking my heart. Ever since

Hawthorne seduced, raped and nearly killed me, Mike hasn't been sympathetic, he's been judgmental."

"I'm so sorry. I want you to know that none of us has judged you for one minute. The man was a psychopath and seducing and destroying is their specialty. I should know seeing as how I had to deal with the horror of what Johnnie and Tommy Black did to me."

The girls hugged each other tightly each reliving their own pain and the pain of their friends.

"You were about as much to blame as a rock. The guy's a confirmed psychopath and serial killer," said Jerry as he opened the door and pushed in next to Kendall.

From behind the wheel CJ turned to the back. "Ready ladies and gents?"

A knock sounded on the driver's window. CJ hit the button and the window went down revealing Joe and Andy.

"Can you fit two more?" asked Joe.

CJ looked at them with a knowing smile. "U'm the truck right in front of us has only two people in it and we have five."

"That's two too many for me," said Andy.

"Open the back hatch and we can ride back there." Joe walked to the back of the suburban and pounded on the window.

"Ok! Now stop beating up the truck and get in!"

The hatch opened and the two men climbed in. Joe pulled the hatch closing the door and smiled.

Kipp opened the driver's door then leaned in over CJ. "So let me get this straight. There's a truck with two people sitting right in front of us, but you all are packed in here like sardines?"

"You got it," said Andy.

Kipp made a shooing motion with his hands. "Get over girl this old dog is driving." He laughed a clear, easy going laugh, that sounded like beautiful music to the team.

The truck carrying Mike and Lana pulled away first.

"Where ever they are going, I vote on not joining them," said Kendall.

"Have no fear, I've gotten the clear..."

"Yeah, yeah Kipp we know and Under Dog is here," said CJ.

"No serious we are cleared to head to the airport. Our bags are already there and any debriefing can be done on

Skype or some kind of thingie like that," said Kipp.

"Thingie, huh? Wow I'm impressed, you really are moving into the new millennium boss," said Jerry from the farthest back of the truck.

Squished like sardines the members of the Midnight Riders, plus one Agent Debbie Crane, drove away leaving the memory of the greatest sadist they'd ever encountered behind.

"So got room for another agent on this team?" Debbie Crane looked around the packed truck.

The women all nodded and said "Hell yes!"

The men simply wondered just how the ice queen had thawed so quickly.

# CHAPTER THIRTY

Mike and Lana huddled together in the back seat of the FBI SUV, alone except for the unknown agent driving.

"Makes it pretty clear I'm no longer welcome on the Midnight Rider's Team," said Mike glumly as he shook his head.

"I'm sorry Mike. I wish we'd waited until you worked things out with Kendall. I hate myself for hurting her. She's an awesome person and she deserves better than how we've treated her," said Lana.

"So what? Now you're a Kendall supporter too?" He unwrapped his arm from the woman beside him and leaned back to look in her eyes.

Lana glared at him, fire flashing in her green eyes. "Don't you get it. I'm just like Kendall now! Everything and more that he did to her, he did to me! I won't be alive if Kendall hadn't risked her life to come save me. So go ahead reject me like a piece of shit, just like you did Kendall. Only thing is, I'm going to walk away from you, without so much as a glance back."

Mike inhaled sharply as an unknown emotion, called fear, went coursing through his every pore. "Lana I didn't know. I'm so sorry, honey. I could never reject you. I can't lose you." He pulled her into his hard chest.

"Why? I'm no different than Kendall, yet you've been making her pay for the same mistake." Lana buried her head in his chest. "Until you make it right with her, we can go no further romantically."

Mike inhaled her scent and tickled his nose on her short shaggy hair. "I know you're right and I promise I will. She needs some time to decompress from all of this first. I realized what an ass I've been while sitting in lock up with nothing to do, but think. I've got a lot to make up for and I promise you Lana, I will."

Lana hugged him tighter. "Let's go home." She gave the driver her address and they drove away from the scene and into what they both hoped was a new and brighter life together.

## CHAPTER THIRTY-ONE

Kendall leaned back in the private jet's plush chair and promptly fell sound asleep.

Jerry smiled, sitting next to her, as little snuffles of snoring came from her lips. "I don't know about you all, but I am so happy this case is finally closed."

"I wonder if we will ever find out what happened to Gail Gas, aka Chris Hawthorne?" said Kipp. He glanced at Bobbie and CJ with raised eye brows.

Bobbie shrugged.

CJ smacked her lips together. "Guess some things just remain mysteries."

Andy reached over and took her hand in his. "One mystery was solved during this case."

CJ looked up at him. "Oh really and what was that?"

"That you three are like Lucy, Emma Peel and Samantha combined and I love you madly." Andy reached over and pulled CJ to him. He kissed her deeply. "I don't know what I would have done if anything had happened to you."

"I hope it's just me you love." CJ kissed him back smiling as his face turned beat red.

"Of course only you. I mean really how could you..."

"Oh shut up and kiss her, please!" Oliver said laughing.

The flight passed quickly between sleeping and easy talk amongst friends, thicker than thieves. It landed a few hours later at Teterboro Airport.

"Come on sleepy head, wake up," Jerry gently shook Kendall's shoulder.

Her eyelids flashed open and she jumped up, fists in the air, fear and something else written on her face.

Jerry stood up. "Easy Kendall. I'm sorry I scared you. I tried to wake you up slowly so this didn't happen." He looked at her face. "However, upon seeing your face, I'm glad I woke you, cause what is written there says that never again will you let another person hurt you."

Kendall exhaled sharply and put her fisted hands down. Her racing heart gradually slowed to normal. "You can say that again my friend. Next time you do that I might not be so gentle."

Jerry laughed as did the rest of the team. "Now that I can't wait to see."

The team slowly gathered their belongings and exited the plane, thanking the captain and first officer as they exited.

"I for one can't wait to get home to a certain yellow lab I miss more than life itself." Kendall practically ran to the waiting MRI black Suburban. She opened the hatch and threw her gear in then jumped into the back seat. "Come on, put some life in those steps!"

"I think somebody is back in form," said Kipp.

"Thank God," said Bobbie.

They all piled into the big Suburban and headed for base.

"You know I've always wanted to write a book and after this case I've got some pretty good fodder," said Kendall.

"Fodder, huh. Well with that vocabulary it will be sure to be a smash," said Jerry.

"Seriously I'm going to do it. The life coach said writing can be very cathartic. I may very well be a world famous writer soon." Kendall leaned back in the seat, smiling.

"The names have been changed to protect the innocent. All except Mike Garcia, his name can stay the same," said CJ.

"True dat," said Joe.

"I never need to see his face again as far as I am concerned," said Bobbie.

"Same here," said Bert.

"Hey guys, I really love you and appreciate you supporting me, but let's face it, I have blame in how things went too. One of these days Mike and I will have to sit down and have a long talk. I don't ever want to work with him again or be involved with him, but I don't want to hate him either. Hate will destroy me." Kendall sighed then smiled as her house came into view.

"I'm home! I can't wait to see Bela and take a long, long hot bath."

"Need some company for that long, long hot bath," Jerry said sexily."

Kendall wacked him on the arm and opened the door before the truck even stopped. "In your dreams Knight!"

She got out and ran towards the house, just as Bela, burst through the doggie door and headed her way.

"Bela girl!" Kendall hugged the gentle giant who leaped and knocked her flat onto her back.

"I missed you," said Kendall as Bela filled her face with wet doggie kisses.

Bobbie grabbed Bela's collar. "Let your mom get up girl."

Kipp carried Kendall's bags into the house and set them down on the floor. She walked in behind him with Bela and Bobbie trailing.

"Are you going to be ok here by yourself?" he said, concern filling his voice.

"For the first time since this nightmare began, I can honestly say, I will be fine. There isn't anyone left to hurt me. I'm safe, thanks to all of you!"

She held out her arms and a giant group hug ensued as each member of the team walked inside. Bela squeezed into the middle, next to her mom's leg.

"Thank you my wonderful tribe of awesome people! I'm going to dedicate the book to you."

Kipp laughed and the rest of the group burst out the same as the hug broke up.

"No seriously, I'm writing a book. Gonna be some romance, some mystery and most of all the most amazing friends in the whole wide world." Kendall pet Bela's head.

"Gotta go," Kipp leaned in and kissed Kendall on the cheek. "I'm sure it will be a great success."

Jerry was next. "You should call it - Knight to the Rescue."

Bobbie pushed Jerry out of the way. "Yeah, that will sell." She hugged her best friend and kissed her cheek. "We did it," she whispered.

CJ rubbed Kendall's back. "I'll call you later and make sure everything is fine."

The rest of the team waved their good byes and walked out the door.

She waved out the big picture window as the Suburban backed out of the driveway and faded from view.

"I am going to write a book Bela girl and it is gonna be a hum dinger. I've already got the title - Kendall Rose and the Midnight Riders. "What do you think?"

The yellow lab gently grabbed hold of Kendall's shirt and guided her over to her special cabinet.

Kendall laughed and opened the door, grabbing several biscuits and a bone. "Here you go girl."

After a quick dinner, a long, long hot bath and several well meaning phone calls, Kendall lay down on fresh sheets and fell asleep before her head even hit the pillow.

The End

Preview of the next Kendall Rose Mystery

## A SIMPLE CASE OF POISON.

She looked down at her shoes or rather boots with four inch heels, black in color with black pants tucked in snuggly. Holding out her arm she admired the silky deep turquoise shirt that went down to her thighs and was nicely pulled in at the waist by a sparking jeweled belt.

"Wow, I really clean up nice. I'm liking this dream."

Her head went up at the sound of someone calling her name.

"Kendall Rose over here! Yoo hoo," said a rotund woman holding several books in her arms."Please have a seat behind your table as the guests will be entering soon."

Kendall looked around the large room, full of famous authors. Some were sitting behind their tables with books on them Others milled about waiting for the crowd to enter.

"What the heck is going on?" Kendall said, not to quietly.

The rotund lady quickly walked over to her and wrapped her arm around her shoulders, guiding her behind one of the tables with books on them.

She looked down and there in the flesh sat her book! It's cover glistened in the light and there at the bottom of the cover was her name, Kendall Rose. She'd done it! Written her very own book!

She sat down blissfully basking in the accolades of other authors who stopped by and then the readers who eagerly wanted her to sign their copy of her book.

My book. She glanced down at the title once again that read...

Suddenly shouts of alarm went up. The rotund woman grabbed her by the cuff of her jacket and practically pulled her out of her chair.

"Quick! Palmer Mandrakes, author of suspense and mystery has collapsed! They need you over there now!"

Kendall broke free of her grip and bent down to get her purse under the table. She pulled it out, unzipped it and lifted out a pair of latex-free medical gloves that she always carried for an emergency. She slide on gloves as the rotund woman yelled for her to "hurry!"

"Keep your shorts on sister! It's only a dream after all." Kendall pushed the purse back under the table and got up, following behind the woman who began pushing through a gathering crowd.

"Paramedic Kendall Rose is coming! Out of the way!" yelled her escort.

Kendall burst through the crowd and there at her feet lay a handsome blonde man, bleeding from the mouth and obviously unconscious or worse yet, dead.

She dropped to her knees, landing next to the man's side and felt for a pulse. It was slow, very slow. "Who called 911?"

A man raised his hand. "I did."

"Good! Now who can tell me what happened?" Kendall looked the man up and down for signs of trauma. The only thing she noted was a mild nose bleed.

"He'd just finished eating some soup and happily sat down to sign books. His fans are very eager you know..."

Kendall held up her hand. "Please get to the point! I need to know what happened."

The lady, obviously his assistant nodded. "Yes, yes. Sorry about that I do go on at times...:

She stopped when Kendall rolled her eyes and bent down sniffing the man's breath. "I smell almonds. Does anyone else smell almonds?"

Just then, a pair of turnout gear, covered legs, knelt beside her. She looked up into the deepest blue eyes she'd ever seen.

"What's going on?"asked a handsome firefighter, with silvery- gray hair and a rockin sexy body. This dream was getting better by the second.

"I'm a paramedic in NJ, my name's Kendall Rose. I'm not sure what is going on. I'm here signing my books and someone came to get me because this man collapsed. He's got a very slow pulse and I believe I smell almonds. He just finished eating a bowl of soup. Ah shit!"

The famous author started to vomit. Kendall and the firefighter rolled him on his side, so the puke rolled out and not back down, obscuring his airway.

"Someone get me a towel!" Kendall looked up into the eyes of the crowd. "Now please!"

Seconds later a roll of paper towels fell by her hands. Quickly Kendall pulled off several sheets then bent down and wiped the vomit off the man's face and out of his airway.

"Looks clear. Let's get him on his back and check for a pulse," said the firefighter. With Kendall's help, he rolled the man onto his back.

"My name is Tank," said the drop dead, out of some kind of romance novel, firefighter. Heck, her dream was getting better by the second, except for the famous writer hanging on to his life by a thread.

"Good to meet you. I was saying before he vomited, that I smell sweet almonds. Now, I smell it even stronger, with the puke on the floor." She shuddered.

He nodded his silver- haired head. "I smell it too."

A pair of solid blue pants with a yellow strip down the side arrived next and squatted down, beside Kendall and Tank.

"Smell that?" said Tank.

"Sure do," said the cop, just as the famous and now dead writer, took his last breath. "Seal the doors! This man's been murdered!"

Coming soon.

www.ingramcontent.com/pod-product-compliance
Lightning Source LLC
Chambersburg PA
CBHW070923130626
46555CB00001B/256